SHATTERED LIVES

VINEET VERMA

VINEET
VERMA

This book is a work of fiction. All the characters and events portrayed in this novel are fictitious. Similarities to real people, places, or events are coincidental.

Copyright 2024 Vineet Verma

Cover design by Elizabeth Mackey/elizabethmackey.com

All rights reserved. The distribution of this book without permission is a theft of the author's intellectual property. If you would like permission to use material from the book (other than for review purposes), please contact sayhello@vineetvermaauthor.com. Thank you for your support of the author's rights.

Contents

PROLOGUE

Something horrendous is coming my way. I sensed it the moment I awoke this morning — the same feeling I had the day Mom died. My chest feels heavy, and a piercing headache is gathering strength. I've tried to ignore the unease all day, but the sense of foreboding reaches a crescendo as I continue knocking on Annie's door. *Where the hell is she?* When I spoke to her yesterday, she'd assured me she would be home today. I call her once again, but no luck. A flurry of texts. No response. My breathing quickens. My stomach churns. I fear the worst.

A final series of knocks.

Nothing.

I wait ten seconds, my heart sinking further with every tick.

Frantic, I fish out the key she gave me a while back after I insisted, only to be used in emergencies. I struggle to steady my trembling hands and fit the key in the slot, but once I do, it turns without a hitch and the door opens.

I smell pizza. Fresh. I step inside and glance towards the kitchen. The box on the countertop confirms what my nose already told me. So she must be home, or must have been at some point to have ordered her favorite meal. Not something she would have done if she had planned on ending things. My disquiet eases a bit, but not entirely.

It's eerily quiet, with no one in sight. I want to call out to her, but my throat has gone dry and words refuse to emerge. I hustle around the apartment, desperately hoping to discover her alive and well. Perhaps I'll find her huddled in a corner, engrossed in a thriller novel, oblivious to the world around her. The kitchen, the bedroom, even the closets — she's nowhere to be found. Maybe that's a good sign, I try to convince myself, but it's a futile effort.

There's only one place I haven't looked, so I hurry towards the bathroom. It's only a short distance from where I'm standing, but in my agitated state it seems like I'm running a marathon.

The door is open a crack, with a sliver of light streaming through. A strong lavender scent hits me, along with a hint of bleach, even before I enter. I push the door open wide. The first thing I see is the bathtub, filled to the brim with water. A step closer and I lay eyes on the naked, still body underneath the surface. My heart's hammering inside my chest now. I rush to her, hoping I'm not too late.

"Noo, noo, noo." I've finally found my voice.

My hands shake as I make a clumsy effort to unplug the drain and pull her head out of the water. Water splashes out of the tub, spilling on my jeans and shoes. *Glug, glug, glug.* The water starts draining. She's not breathing. No pulse either. I'm panicking now, though I can't afford to. I take in a few deep breaths, trying to suppress the urge to throw up. Maybe I can still revive her. I try to drag her out, but she's heavy.

Before I can make another attempt, I realize I should call 911 first, so I dial and put the phone on speaker, placing it on the sink. It's a struggle, but I manage to haul her out and lay her on the floor. My muscles burn with the effort. Sweat oozes out of my every pore. Down on my knees, I've just completed a round of CPR when someone answers.

"911, what's your emergency?"

"My sister, she's … she's not breathing."

The rest of the call is a blur as I answer the dispatcher's questions while trying to resuscitate her. I'm losing hope — and my nerve. My little sis isn't responding. The dispatcher assures me they're sending help right away. She instructs me to continue with the CPR. So I keep going, knowing deep inside that it's a lost cause. But I can't afford to lose her. I must keep trying. I must not give up.

1

DANIEL

She's cheating on me. I'm sure of it. Learning this brutal truth about my wife of twenty years is like a punch in the gut, a blow to the head, a kick in the groin — all at the same time. I'm hurting. The wound runs deep, as you would expect when your partner drives a knife through your heart and betrays you. This was supposed to be a joyous day, another celebration of my career as an author, but I feel no joy. Instead, I'm dead inside. It's ironic, because it's as if Heather and I have become a dysfunctional couple from one of my novels.

I'm not one of those husbands who's always suspicious of his wife, wondering whether she's seeing anyone behind my back. Until now she had my complete trust — I never tried to snoop on her emails or her phone, never followed her around town or hired a PI to dig up dirt on her. It's just pure chance that I found out about the affair.

On my way to an errand yesterday afternoon, something compelled me to deviate from the usual route and drive down First Street. It's a shabby part of town, even without any of the homeless encampments that dot other parts of San Jose. I tend to avoid it, preferring to travel through more pleasant parts of the city.

Sleepytime Motel is one of the dumpy establishments that line this section of the street, with an uncovered parking lot and rooms that open onto the lot. Stopped at a light adjacent to the motel and with nothing better to do, I was surveying the property when Heather exited a room. I blinked thrice, convinced that my eyes were misleading me. But no — she was still there, as real as the sun blazing overhead. I couldn't fathom why she was at a motel, especially a fleabag like this one, considering that we can afford much better. Her tousled hair and furtive glances indicated she'd been a naughty girl. Thankfully, it didn't seem like she had spotted me.

The sighting threw my insides into tumult, my mind flitting through all the men in our circle, trying to figure out who was the Brutus to my Caesar — friends, acquaintances, other dads, but none of them seemed like candidates. It made me wonder, though. What kind of scoundrel would make the candidate list? Perhaps it was an old flame, someone I didn't know. A college sweetheart or a high school crush that she had reconnected with. My stomach churned at the thought.

More questions followed. How long had this deception been going on? Was it a fling or something more serious? I envisioned worst-case scenarios — what if she wanted a divorce? My heart ached for my children. Jonas might withstand the tsunami, but Joyce — that sensitive soul — at fifteen, she's smack in the middle of her turbulent teenage years. She might buckle under.

I continued down the rat hole of misery, finally ending at the most important question — *why?* Why was she doing this? My mind came up blank. I was so agitated that I couldn't sleep last night, tossing and turning, debating whether I was a wimp for not confronting Heather, for striving to avoid conflict. She, on the other hand, slept like a baby, like she does every night. *Had she lost her conscience?*

But I'm a professional, and as much as I want to scamper home, down a bottle of Macallan, draw the curtains and curl up in bed, I've suppressed my emotions for now. I'm in my car, in the Plentiful Books parking lot. The book signing begins at 1:00 p.m. There's still plenty of time.

2

—·—

DANIEL

Her Darkest Fears is my twelfth book, and like all my novels that preceded it — all thrillers — it's a thumping success. That level of success means I'm invited for signings at bookstores around the country. Today is one such event. Though I've done this many times over the course of my career, until today I've been excited every single time. I don't take my achievements for granted, appreciating the fact that my fans adore me and are eager to meet me in person. And Plentiful Books holds a special place in my heart. It's where I had my first signing twenty-one years ago — for my debut novel, *Righteous Kill*.

Bookstores are reader heaven. And cozy indie bookstores like Plentiful Books are top-tier heaven, if such a thing exists. Stopping as soon as I enter the store, I gawk at the books on display. I'd like nothing better than to stroll around, browse the shelves, and inhale the aroma of fresh, unread books as I try to escape my woes. But I have work to do. As always, I'm a bit nervous. The key difference between my first book signing and this one is that I'm a lot more confident now, which is not surprising given my accomplishments since then.

I lift my gaze from the books to take in the rest of the store. It's packed. It's a lovely sight, and the owner, Brandon, looks excited, but it fails to energize me, given the concerns weighing on my mind. He welcomes me inside enthusiastically. Soon he's introducing me to the audience, and the applause comforts me. I muster a smile and a few words of gratitude before getting down to business.

I breeze through my reading on autopilot and plant myself at the table as the readers line up eagerly, copies of *Her Darkest Fears* in hand. I get through them one by one, signing the books while making small talk. There are paperbacks and hardcovers, and I reserve my widest smiles for the ones who purchase the hardcovers, because I have a soft spot for the hardbacks, dust jacket and all. The enthusiasm from my fans and the conversations with them help me settle into a rhythm.

An older man, probably around the age my father would have been if he were alive today, tells me how he has read every one of my novels cover to cover, and he's looking forward to devouring this one tonight. A young woman tells me her husband's a huge fan, but he couldn't make it since he had to work. She's going to surprise him with a copy. Lucky guy.

"How about you? Have you read any of my work?" I ask.

She shrugs, looking a bit embarrassed. "Sorry, I don't read." Then she cracks a grin. "But I'd watch the Netflix series if they ever make one."

I chuckle and sign the book before handing it back to her. Yeah, I'd be thrilled if someone produced a movie or show based on one of my books. She mouths a thank-you as she leaves.

As she departs, I spot a woman further down the queue. Dark hair falling to her shoulders, enticing eyes, and a body that's slender with curves in all the right places. In short, a stunner. I have a hard time getting through the next few readers, because my heart's thumping and I can't wait for the woman to approach. My mind wanders, imagining what it would be like to hold her in my arms, to place my lips on hers, and it lifts my spirits.

It's wrong, I know, but these are just thoughts. Not that I wouldn't be justified in acting on them, considering the mischief Heather's been up to. Speaking of Heather, I wonder what she's doing right now. Is she in bed with her lover again? There was a time when she would accompany me to signings. Even the children came along when they were younger, but they got busy with their own lives once they hit their teens. Heather dropped out around the same time they did. Now it's only me and my sad self.

Suddenly I feel alone. But I shouldn't feel sorry for myself, because the beauty's beaming as she steps up to my table and places her copy before me. A hardcover. She's gushing, telling me how much she admires my work and how blessed she considers herself to have this opportunity to meet me in person. Up close, there's something familiar about her face and her mannerisms, the way she talks, but I'm sure I've never met her.

"Who do I make it out to?" I ask, as my most charming smile spreads across my face.

"Penelope," she replies. "Penelope Hayek."

"That's a beautiful name."

"Thank you." She blushes, and my heart beats a wee bit faster.

Dear Penelope, it's a pleasure to meet you, I write, before signing it. As I raise my gaze to hand the book back to her, she bends — just enough to give me a generous view of her cleavage. Something stirs inside me.

"I wish you could sign me some time," she whispers with a wink.

I'm sure I landed only a subtle glance at her chest, but she must have caught me gawking. I sense myself turning red — partly because I'm embarrassed, but also because I'm flattered that she's interested. It's an unexpected proposition, and I relish the thought, almost replying with a flirtatious remark of my own, but I restrain myself at the last moment.

"You live close by, Penelope?" I try to sound casual.

"I'm only five minutes from here. And you can call me Pen."

Now that's convenient. Temptation mounts, but a voice inside cautions me to resist.

"See you around, Pen," I say as I place the book in her hands and glance behind her to the next person in the queue. She stays put for an instant, and her face tells me she wasn't expecting this brush-off. But she eventually gets the hint and walks away. I content myself with a glimpse of her swaying hips and images of what might have been before turning my attention to the next fan.

It's ironic how I meet attractive women at signings — women who tempt me to cheat on Heather — considering that's how I met her. It was at this same store and my first-ever signing. Plentiful

Books had been gracious enough to invite me — a struggling, unknown author pushing his first novel. But that's the beauty of indie bookstores. At the time I was published by a small press, having taken that route after rejections from dozens of agents. This was before self-publishing became a thing and opened the floodgates for authors to make their dreams come true.

Only five people showed up at the event. Heather was one of them. I was sinking into depression until she arrived and lit up the place. She flashed me a reassuring smile, as if she could sense what I was going through. Her presence gave me the strength to get through the reading. I guess I did well enough, because some of the other customers in the store stopped to listen to me speak.

Heather was first in line when I moved on to the signing. With her blonde hair and blue eyes she wasn't my type, but there was something arresting about her. A quality that made me want to spend time with her. But I couldn't muster the courage to ask her for her number.

I sold a total of ten copies that day. It didn't make much of an impact on the tepid sales figures, but Brandon assured me he loved the book and he would continue to promote it. It was nice of him to say that, but it didn't help improve my mood. What did help was seeing Heather waiting for me by the door as I packed up my things and exited the store.

"I hope you don't think I'm stalking you," she said, waving my book in her hand, "but this is great."

"You already started reading it?"

"Yeah. At first I thought I'd just read the first page, but it sucked me right in. I'm on page one hundred."

"Wow. You're a fast reader."

"That I am." She directed a stray strand of hair away from her face and behind her ear.

"Any ... any plans for the evening?" I surprised myself by asking, unsure about my next move.

"Other than finishing this? No."

"Join me for coffee?" I blurted it out before I could chicken out.

"Sure," she replied, the dimples in her cheeks making me go weak in the knees.

I tumbled into love with her over cappuccinos and slices of banana bread. We talked and talked and talked, sharing our backgrounds, our interests, our dislikes. She told me she was an avid supporter of indie stores and had just come to browse when she saw the sign for my event. Having never attended a live author event, she decided to give it a shot. Lucky me.

Based on those first hundred pages, she predicted that *Righteous Kill* would be a bestseller. I didn't believe her at the time, modestly waving away the heaps of praise she laid on me. But there was truth to what she said, because sales picked up soon after, thanks to word-of-mouth. By the time we married a year later, I was a moderately successful author on his way to releasing his second novel. By the third one, I had better agents and publishers reaching out to me. Careerwise, there was no looking back after that. Daniel Geraldi, bestselling author, that's what they started calling me, causing my chest to swell with pride. To this day, I'm convinced

Heather's my lucky charm, and I owe my success to her presence by my side.

The next fan pulls me back to the present, and I continue with the small talk and signing books. It's another hour before the queue dries up and I get to wrap up. A successful day by any measure. I should be delighted, but this event was just a distraction, and now that it's over, all I can think about is Heather and her lover in that motel room.

3

DANIEL

It's a short drive back home, and I'm easing the car into the driveway when I spot our next-door neighbor Rhonda emerging from her *casa* with her golden retriever, Bruno. I've heard "When I Was Your Man" streaming through her windows often enough to guess who she named the dog after. Rhonda's around my age, but she's single, having never married. It's just Bruno and her. I've envied her single life for the longest time — she does whatever she likes, whenever she likes, without a care in the world. It irked me a lot more during those early years with our kids, when we struggled with sleepless nights, tantrums, and the like while she partied hard, went for long morning runs, and slept in on the weekends, even though she did help us with our burdens every now and then.

In spite of the envy, we've shared a pleasant relationship from the beginning, except for a couple of recent hiccups. The first one was a while back, on a night when Heather and I were getting frisky in the living room. The children were already in bed, so we figured we were safe. We were kissing, and I was undressing her when I was startled by a face in one of the windows. I rushed towards the peeping Tom, but they disappeared before I could reach the window. In the semi-darkness outside I saw the figure sprinting out of our driveway and turning right. Based on the frame and gait, I'm confident it was Rhonda, but Heather thinks that's not possible. Rhonda would never do such a thing, she insisted. I never mustered enough courage to bring it up with our neighbor, and I tried to put the incident out of my mind, but it still sulks in a corner.

The second hiccup was my fault. A few weeks ago Bruno blundered by sniffing me and licking my hand, and I lost my temper. Now, it's not that I don't like dogs. They can be adorable, golden retrievers in particular. But I'm unable to ignore the feeling that they're dirty and carry germs. I can't bring myself to pet them or allow them to make physical contact with me in any way. If not for my resistance, we would have adopted a dog by now — Joyce has been clamoring for one since she was three. Thankfully, Bruno helps fill that need, so she's not as adamant as she would have been.

When Bruno licked me, it triggered me. Under normal circumstances I would have let it go, but it was a particularly stressful time in my life, and I was overwhelmed with personal issues and publishing deadlines. I yelled at Bruno and almost hit him before better sense prevailed. It was enough to have him cowering in a corner. Not surprisingly, Rhonda was miffed. She's been a bit frosty with me since then.

As I step out of the car, she plasters a forced smile. I force one of my own.

"Hi, Rhonda," I say as I hurry towards my front door, not expecting her to engage.

"So, I read *Husbands in Peril*."

I freeze in my tracks. *Husbands in Peril* was my tenth novel, an experiment which did quite well. I departed from my usual dark themes and explored a lighter kind of thriller — no one died, and I sprinkled a lot more humor throughout. I had a blast working on it. Now Rhonda has uttered words that would drive any author up the wall due to the extreme and varied emotions they evoke. On the one hand, it's comforting to know that someone found my work compelling enough to spend time and money on it. It's satisfying to know that my novels have an audience. But it's also scary. *What if she hated it?*

I turn to face her, and from her expression I predict she's going to rip the book to shreds, especially considering our Cold War. I wait with bated breath, unable to speak. It's only one reader and feedback that probably will not matter in the grand scheme of things, but I'm as nervous as an Oscar nominee hearing the words, "And the Oscar goes to ..."

Rhonda takes her time, as if she knows that every second I wait is torture for me, and she's relishing the thought. Bruno's stare tells me he hated the book.

"Interesting plot. I loved seeing those men getting their asses kicked by the women for a change. I'm so sick of reading books with weak female protagonists suffering abuse by some thick-headed guy."

I let out the breath I've been holding. That's a relief. But I sense a *but* coming.

"But the ending sucked."

And there it is. I detect a smirk on her visage — she's enjoying this.

"What was wrong with it?"

"It made no sense. I'm not sure how you justify what Andrea did. I felt it was a lazy conclusion to an otherwise entertaining story. All along I was thinking, this is a five-star read. Now I'm not so sure. Three stars, maybe."

Ouch. I don't know how to respond. This is the first time I've had a reader give me such brutal feedback in person. I've received negative reviews before, of course, but that's all online. The buffer helps. The comments hurt for an instant, but over the years I've learned to brush those off and focus on the positive. But this — this pain is lingering. Besides, I know Rhonda's right. I did rush the ending and wrap up the story with a bow just so I could meet my publisher's deadline. If I'd had more time I would have done a better job. Not that it mattered, because the book was a huge success anyway. So successful that my agent and publisher have suggested I write another one in the same vein.

I shrug. "Thanks for giving it a shot."

"I'll be reading your latest one next."

"Great," I reply as I turn towards the front door. Hopefully she loves that one. The thought of hearing another review from her makes me jittery.

Having survived Rhonda, I enter my house. No one's home. Once again, I wonder what Heather is up to, but I push those thoughts out of my head before they take a dark turn. I grab a beer from the fridge and head over to my office, my sanctuary. As much as I enjoy book signings, it's exhausting work, and I need some time to unwind.

My den is well-appointed. There's a massive copper desk and a plush Herman Miller chair where I do all my writing. The desktop is sparse, with only my laptop, docking station, keyboard, mouse, and monitor, and a couple of Moleskine notebooks and pens for taking notes. A bowl of candy graced the desk at one time. The idea was to reward myself with an occasional piece as I hit writing milestones. *Bad idea.* Soon I was having to replenish the bowl daily, so it had to go.

Some potted plants are scattered around the room — Heather's touch, and then there's my pride and joy — the bookshelf that covers the entire wall opposite the desk. I've stocked it with everything from first editions of some classics to every single story published by Agatha Christie, my idol. One of the rows has all the books from Ed McBain's 87th Precinct series. I love picking up a book at random and admiring it, enjoying its texture, opening it and inhaling. The last bit I only do when the office door's shut and I'm alone. The couple of times that Heather and the kids saw me do that, they stared like I was indulging in some weird fetish. *Isn't that something every booklover does?*

I sink into the chair and check my email inbox. Over a hundred unread messages. I constantly debate the merits of hiring an assistant to handle my fan mail. On the one hand, I fear doing so will take away the personal touch and put a distance between me and my fans, but replying to everyone chews up time that could be better spent writing. As I scan the list, one message stands out. The subject says *Thank you for today!*, and the sender's name is Penelope. It was sent a couple of hours ago. I open the email.

> Hi Daniel,
>
> I just wanted to thank you for signing my book today! It was so exciting meeting you in person. I still can't believe it happened. I have been holding the book and admiring your autograph ever since I got home.
>
> Best,
>
> Pen

Her note evokes memories of our brief encounter. I picture her standing in front of me as I run my gaze over her beautiful body. The email is innocuous enough, and I wonder whether I misinterpreted what happened between us. Perhaps it was my imagination. I arrest my thoughts before they drift into forbidden areas.

> Hi Pen,

It was a pleasure meeting you. Thank you so much for taking the time to come, and for purchasing a copy. It's the encouragement from fans like you that keeps me going. I hope you enjoy the book!

Cheers,

Daniel

I move on to other emails, most of which are similar in nature. I spend some time answering those. Pen's response arrives by the time I'm done.

BTW, here's the tattoo you were admiring.

There's an attachment this time. I open it to see a mermaid tattoo. The picture has enough context to tell me I'm looking at her cleavage. *Is she flirting again?* Why else would she send me such an image? On the other hand, if she thinks I was staring at her tattoo, at least she doesn't think I'm a pervert who was drooling over her breasts. I'm not sure how to respond. I take a shot at it after giving it some thought.

It's a beautiful tattoo. You're so brave to get one. I don't think I could handle that pain.

Short and sweet. This time I wait for her to reply. It doesn't take long.

I have more!

It's like we're texting, the brief messages going back and forth so quickly.

> *What kind?*

I pause, debating whether I should type what's on my mind. Then I add it, because it's a question any curious mind would have.

> *And where?*

Her response is almost instantaneous.

> *Of course you want to know where … ;)*

Now my imagination is running wild. I picture tattoos in intimate locations on her body. I picture her in my office, doing a strip tease and revealing each one, reveling in the attention and the joy it gives me. The heat of shame runs over me, and I feel dirty, because this is like I'm cheating on Heather. But another voice inside me insists it's okay — Heather is already cheating on me anyway. There's nothing wrong with what I'm doing. In fact, it's justified. I slam my laptop shut and hurry out of the office before temptation takes me further down a road I should not go.

4

DANIEL

He lies at the bottom of the stairs while I stand nearby, staring, fearful at first, then relieved once I'm convinced he's never going to get up again. I muster enough courage to step towards him, and the moment my body relaxes, he moves. A twitch of the fingers at first, followed by full arm movement as he opens his eyes. Then a swift motion that gets him back on his feet. He takes in his surroundings before glaring at me. I'm trembling now, concerned about what he'll do next. Seconds later he marches in my direction. I shrink back in terror. Then he's right in front of me, the intensity of his gaze burning my entire body. He raises his hand to strike, and I try to dodge the blow.

I wake up with a start, still groggy. It's dark. The bed is warm and cozy, but I'm uncomfortable. It takes me a few seconds to realize I had another nightmare — the same one that has plagued me since my teenage years.

I glance at the other half of the bed. Heather's sound asleep, her breathing relaxed. No nightmares ruining her beauty sleep.

We made love before going to bed. She initiated it. It felt dirty. I wasn't sure why she wanted me, and I'm even more unsure why I complied. As we indulged our urges, I tried to block out images of her and her mystery lover, replacing them with a montage of Pen and her tattooed body. In the end, we were both satisfied, and we drifted into sleep, though I had questions swirling in my head.

The same questions plague me now, but sleep is weighing me down. I place my head back on the pillow and watch my philandering wife until I can't keep my eyes open any longer.

5

—·—

DANIEL

It's the morning after the signing. Heather and I are in the kitchen enjoying breakfast and coffee. Well, at least Heather's enjoying — I'm just ensuring my belly is full. She looks content, but the questions that were left unanswered last night are tormenting me. *Am I being paranoid?* Surely I am, because why else would she want me if she already has a lover? Perhaps I'm mistaken and she was at the motel for some other reason. Or has she figured out that I know, and the sex was a ploy to allay my suspicions? I can't make up my mind about it. I was guilty of thinking about Pen while we were having sex. *Was Heather thinking about her paramour too when I touched her?*

What she's doing is wrong. It violates everything our marriage stands for. I should hate her, be consumed by rage at this injustice, but I don't feel any of that. I'm numb, in a way. Perhaps numb is not the right word. I fear losing her, because I can't imagine a life without her. Instead, I wonder whether I've pushed her into a corner. I know I haven't been very attentive to her in the last few years. Having children didn't help, but now that they're all grown up, I should have the time and energy for Heather. But I've been brushing her off in favor of my writing commitments. Am I being too aggressive, shooting for one book release a year? We're financially comfortable and don't need the money. Perhaps if I ease up on work and devote more time to my wife, she won't feel compelled to run into another man's arms. It's still not too late. At least I hope it isn't.

"So, what did Rhonda want with you? I hope it wasn't another spat about Bruno," Heather asks.

How does she know I spoke to Rhonda?

My surprise clearly shows, because Heather arches her eyebrow and breaks into a sneaky grin. "I have my sources."

"It was a weird conversation, for sure. She said she read *Husbands in Peril* and kinda sorta liked it."

"Really?"

"Yes. And what's even more interesting is she plans to read *Her Darkest Fears*."

"Huh. Interesting indeed." She pauses before continuing. "Well, good for you. Another fan won't hurt." She gives me a peck on the lips. "I'm going to hop into the shower."

She dumps her plate and coffee mug in the sink and heads upstairs. I might be wrong, but I sensed she wasn't happy about me talking to Rhonda. I wonder why. It's not like Rhonda and I are flirting or even remotely interested in each other. I stick around at the breakfast nook, killing time on my phone.

Soon Heather's back. She plants another soft kiss on my lips and tells me she's heading out for an errand. The kiss is comforting until I notice her yellow dress, hair, and makeup. She's stunning. Tempting enough that I don't want her to leave. I have an urge to lead her up to the bedroom and continue where we left off last night. But the impulse disappears because I know this isn't the look she carries for simple errands. My suspicions about her affair are rekindled.

I hop into my car as soon as she drives off. Following her is not easy; she'll spot me if I get too close, so I keep my distance. We drive for a few minutes, and when she turns onto First Street, my heart sinks. There's only one place she could be going. Soon enough, she enters the parking lot of the same motel. I remain outside and watch as she gets out of her car and climbs up the stairs. She knocks on the door of a different room. The knock is answered in an instant, and she disappears inside. I was unable to see who welcomed her. I park on the street and wait, every moment consumed by thoughts of her in bed with this anonymous lover. It's tearing me up inside.

It isn't until two hours later that she emerges from the room, her hair tousled once again. She appears content. Happy. Whoever was in there with her showed her a fabulous time. *Better than what I can offer?* I fear the answer.

Heather exits the parking lot. I continue to wait, curious about her paramour. Another ten minutes and the door to the room opens again. A young man, probably in his late twenties, emerges. He's handsome, and he's familiar, but I can't place him. He seems to be in excellent shape — better than me for sure. I'm envious. Filled with rage, the way I would have expected when I first learned of this indiscretion. A part of me wants to confront him, but what good will that do? I let him drive off in his beat-up Accord, resisting the urge to follow.

I grab the newspaper once I get home and settle into my favorite chair. I didn't get a chance to read it this morning, and now I need something to comfort myself. The sensation of newsprint in my hands, the scent, the crinkle of paper, it's soothing. There's so much content available online, but I prefer digesting the news this way. Today, however, depressing news dominates.

There's been another shooting, which has become almost a daily occurrence in this country. But this one hits harder than others, because it was right here in San Jose — too close to home. It wasn't even a mass shooting at a mall or at an event. A man shot dead his ex-wife and five-year-old daughter in their apartment because he didn't want to pay child support anymore. Two innocent lives lost so cheaply. What a monster. But who am I to judge? Some memories surface and make me nauseous. I let the feeling pass. No point dredging up the past. What's done is done.

The bad news doesn't stop there. Another local woman is missing — the fifth one in the last five months. All these women were jogging on trails when they disappeared. I take comfort in the fact that neither Heather nor Joyce are runners.

Joyce. The very thought of her brightens my mood. She's a sweetheart. Kind, loving. She's in that awkward teenage phase, but clichéd as it may sound, I'm sure my little duckling will grow up to be a beautiful swan like her mother. She's also a talented soccer player. And while she's an average student academically, she's smart in her own unique way. She wants to be an author, just like me. I've read some of her work, and she has potential. That's a real, impartial critique — I'm not saying this because I'm her father. The best part about her stories is the protagonists — strong, independent women who can hold their own. Clearly, we did something right in the way we raised her.

I continue reading the news about the missing women. The speculation is that it's the work of a serial killer, though none of the bodies have been found yet. This monster already has a name. Not something vicious like Jack the Ripper or The Boston Strangler, or even The Golden State Killer, but a name that evokes fond memories of chocolates — Forest Grump. Once I read the explanation of how this moniker came about, I wasn't sure whether the guy who came up with it was a genius or someone who should be locked away. It's an obvious reference to Forrest Gump, who, as we all know, loved a good run. Forest, because all the victims disappeared from nature trails, somewhat akin to forests. And Grump, because, well, the killer must be royally pissed off to be picking off women like this.

"What's eating you?" Jonas asks as he drops onto the chair opposite mine. I was so engrossed in my thoughts that I didn't hear him come in.

It seems like only yesterday that I held his tiny infant body in my arms, knowing I would do anything to protect him. I often reminisce about the time he was a puffy-eyed toddler, with tears streaming down his cheeks, snot trickling down his nose, going *bee-bee* when he couldn't find his favorite blankie. Now he's eighteen. A handsome lad — strapping six foot two with a muscular build achieved through hard work in the gym, captivating blue eyes like his mother's, floppy blond hair, and a smile that can melt anyone. *How did he grow up so fast?*

Jonas is an amazing athlete and no slouch in academics either. He's headed to Georgia Tech soon to study Computer Science. He makes me proud. I was the geeky kid in school — forgettable when it came to athletic endeavors. Finishing last in every race I've ever run is my trademark. I've dropped more balls than I've caught, struck out more times than I've connected bat with ball. Too scrawny to attempt football; too short for basketball. The list goes on. So it's especially comforting that Jonas excels at sports. I live the jock life vicariously through him.

"Another woman missing," I reply.

"Out running?"

I nod.

"That sucks. I wish they were more careful, though."

"Careful, how? You don't expect them to stop going outdoors, do you?"

He shakes his head. "No, that's not what I meant. But I see so many of them running with earbuds or headphones, listening to loud music. They can't hear what's going on around them. It's so easy for anyone to creep up and nab them. They would have no clue."

"I see your point."

"So, who do you think is doing this?"

"If I knew, the man would be behind bars already."

He rewards me with the grin he reserves for my Dad jokes. "Dad, not that specific. You write all these crime novels. What's this guy's profile?"

It's a good question. I assume the authorities are on it and have some idea of the kind of creep they're looking for, though they haven't shared anything publicly.

"Well, one problem is that we don't know if he's killing them, or he's just holding them captive."

"Let's assume he's killing them."

"Most serial killers are white males. Odds are, he is too. Again, based on statistics, this guy's probably in his late twenties or early thirties."

Jonas considers my response. "You don't think he could be younger?"

"I doubt it. Crimes such as these need a lot of planning and patience. Sorry to say, but it's rare for someone younger to plan that meticulously or have the patience to wait for the right moment. Especially today's generation that expects everything right now."

He shakes his head. "Don't underestimate us, Dad."

"I'm not saying it's not possible, just that it's highly unlikely."

"I guess. Hope they nab this monster soon."

"Me too."

He glances at his watch. "Well, I gotta run. I'm meeting some friends for lunch."

"Have fun. Catch you later."

He departs. I glance at the paper that's still in my hands and figure I can't take any more negative news. Instead, I turn to the leisure section — to the comforting and familiar corner of *Luann*, *Sally Forth*, *Garfield*, and *Zits*. Perhaps I'll give the sudoku or the crossword a shot. Anything to take my mind off the turmoil in the world — and in my life.

6

ANONYMOUS

There's a hole in my heart. A massive void where she once roosted, where she filled me with joy. It's eating me inside. It hurt when Mom passed, but not like this. I've lived my life knowing there would come a day when I would have to bury my parents. But I didn't expect to lose a sibling, certainly not this early. My sister was supposed to outlive me. After losing her, I didn't get out of bed for days, wallowing in misery with the curtains drawn, allowing the darkness to envelop me. I didn't eat. Didn't shower. I'd lost the will to live. Until one morning I saw the light. Realization dawned and I knew what I had to do with my life. It helped haul me out of my miserable existence.

Don't get me wrong — I still miss her. I've got all her stuff — the dirty sheets she last slept in. Her clothes, including the ugly reindeer sweater I'd got her for her last Christmas — the one she claimed she hated. I guess she didn't loathe it as much as she let on, considering she hadn't tossed it. When my heart aches, I grab one of her things and hold it tight. I take in her scent, and for a moment it's as if she never left.

But I don't wallow anymore like I did those first few months. Now that my life has purpose, I'm going all out to fulfill it. It hurts when I miss her, but at least I have something to dull the pain. Whether I'll accomplish my goal or not, I don't know, but what I do know is that I'll do everything it takes to get there. I owe it to myself. And I owe it to her.

7

HEATHER

I'm standing outside our home, relishing the cool morning breeze. Considering how bright the sun is already, I know this won't last. It's going to be a scorcher. My time with Patrick yesterday dominates my thoughts. His hands caressing me, his lips devouring me. The way he explored my body, excited me, pleasured me. *Why isn't it like this with Daniel anymore? Is it him, or is it me?* Or is this what I must resign myself to after two children and twenty years of marriage?

Am I so pathetic that I still crawl back to my husband, hoping to spark some of that magic of old, to experience with him what I feel with Patrick? In spite of everything, I'm convinced Daniel still loves me, though why I still love him after what he has done, it's a mystery to me. Perhaps I'm being too harsh on him, expecting him to perform like a guy almost half his age. But it's not just the pleasure that I crave. I miss spending time together like we used to, and I crave the emotional connection we shared when we made love before. Age is not an excuse for what's lacking here.

But enough of the depressing thoughts. I push Daniel out of my head and think about Patrick again. He's like a breath of fresh air, a welcome distraction from my life. My lips settle into a satisfied smile.

"Looks like someone had an adventurous night."

The comment breaks me out of my reverie. I turn to see Rhonda sporting a mischievous grin. She's sweaty and in running gear, a sign that she has just completed her daily six-mile run. I burn with envy as I survey her svelte figure. Considering the awful shape I'm in, I know I should start running too and shed those extra pounds. No more excuses to skip exercise now that the children are all grown up.

Friend or foe? I'm always unsure about Rhonda. Most of the time she's friendly and seems like a nice person, the kind of neighbor everyone hopes for. But then there are times I get the feeling she's being spiteful — about what, I don't know. Honestly, I'd rather spend time with Bruno than her. At least I know where I stand with Bruno.

"Oh, well." I shrug as I reply, maintaining an air of mystery. There's no way I'm sharing the secret to my happiness.

"It must be wonderful not having to do anything all day."

There she goes again. *Bitch!* The jab stings. It's so difficult to reconcile this version of her with the one who makes us casseroles when we are sick, the one who offers to sign for our packages. One of these days I'll ask Daniel to write a character named Rhonda in his novel and ensure she dies a long, brutal death. Why do women like her do this to other women? We must stick together and respect the choices we make, whether we're pursuing a successful career or tending to the home. Besides, what does she know about life as a parent? Is she even qualified to comment? I want to lash out, scream that she's wrong, but that won't get me anywhere. Instead, I make a measured remark to make my point.

"Yes, it is. After all those years dealing with two children, I've earned it."

She frowns. "Good for ya." She turns to enter her home. Fleeing with her tail between her legs. No comebacks there, huh, Rhonda?

But her barb still rankles. At one time I was a successful real estate agent, consistently ranking in the top ten percent in the country, and on my way up the ladder with greater heights to conquer. Then the kids came. They became my priority. I quit the workforce to take care of them. Now all people see is this plain, pudgy housewife. Patrick's the only one who has been able to scratch the surface and see the beauty within. Or at least he makes me feel like he does. I'm more than a wife and a mother. I'm an accomplished woman — strong and independent, capable of so much more. I must return to work and show these idiots what I've got to offer.

Both Daniel's and my parents have long passed. Neither of us have any siblings. As a result, we don't have any extended family get-togethers like many people do. No raucous Thanksgiving dinners with uncles, aunts and cousins laughing together one minute and arguing over some silly political issue the next. Jonas and Joyce never really knew their grandparents. There are no cousins in their lives — no uncles, no aunts. It saddens me sometimes. That's why

I'd hoped things would be better with Rhonda. That she could be a sister to me and fill that void in my life. That she could be an aunt to the kids. There's some consolation that my children have each other and they always will, long after Daniel and I are gone. That's a huge reason why I wanted at least two kids.

I turn to face the street again. The cool breeze is no more. The sun's shining down hard, and my skin is heating up. How things change within minutes. I glance at the O'Donnells' house across the street. Now, they're a decent family. I'm glad they moved in. And the son is adorable. The only thing I don't like is the security cameras they installed. The cameras capture our house, and I feel we've lost our privacy. I'm always conscious that they can view videos of us outside our home, as well as indoors, if we're not careful to close the blinds. Which reminds me that I have to nag Daniel once again about installing our own cameras. Well, nag isn't the word I'd use — it's more like a gentle reminder, but that's the term he uses when he jokes about it.

The thought that the O'Donnells' cameras might be capturing me right now makes me shudder. I turn around and get back inside. The first thing I do is to shut the blinds that face the street.

8

DANIEL

We're all settled in the living room when the doorbell sounds. It's one of those rare moments when the entire family is together. We did spend a lot of time as a family in the past, but that changed once the kids entered their teen years. Most of the time they stay in their rooms doing whatever it is that teens do these days, only coming down at mealtime. I end up spending more time in the office, writing, more so since discovering what Heather's been up to. Sometimes I miss those chaotic but simpler times.

I amble to the door and open it. There's a small package on the ground. No delivery truck in sight. I pick up the box. No shipping label — just a typed note that says, "From your biggest fan." My heart leaps in delight. A surprise gift for me, I assume. I've received cards and little gifts from fans in the past, but they've all been delivered to my PO box. It's the first time something like this has landed on my doorstep. I'm excited like a child on Christmas morning, wondering what it could be. The package isn't too heavy or too light — it's the weight one would expect for a box this size. I shake it gently, but there's no movement inside.

I wonder who sent it. It hasn't been mailed, so it must be someone who lives close by. While some of my neighbors have claimed to enjoy my work, I don't think any of them loves it so much as to leave me a gift. And why not hand it to me instead of dropping it off like this? And why keep it anonymous? I carry the box to the living room.

"Who was it?" asks Heather before she sees the box in my hands. "Is that my Amazon package?"

I shake my head as I place it on the coffee table.

"Ooh, how exciting. Looks like someone enjoyed your latest," she says once she reads the note.

Jonas and Joyce join us, their interest piqued by this new development.

"Open it, Dad," Joyce chimes in, the enthusiasm in her voice palpable.

We settle on the floor around the table. For a moment I'm bursting with gratitude, delighted that the entire family is celebrating my work. Kinda like those days when they would accompany me to book signings.

"Here goes nothing," I say as I rip off the tape and open the flaps.

Boom!

Joyce screams.

Heather unleashes a shriek.

I'm too stunned to respond. It's a small explosion, more like a balloon popping, but it's accompanied by a thin haze of smoke. That's enough to inject terror into us since it's so unexpected.

"What the fuck!" The f-bomb would have earned Jonas an admonishment under normal circumstances, but I let it slide this time.

The smoke dissipates quickly. I'm horrified to see we're all covered in crimson. Blood. My first thought is that my family is hurt, and it sends a wave of panic through me. The fact that I feel I don't have any injuries is little consolation.

"Are you alright?" I ask, looking from Heather to Jonas to Joyce. They're in shock and probably have the same concerns as me on seeing red everywhere.

"I'm okay," says Heather, her voice meek.

"Me too," replies Joyce.

Jonas nods. I heave a sigh of relief that no one is injured. A closer inspection reveals that it's paint, not blood.

"What kind of sick joke is this?" This time there's an edge to Heather's voice.

"I have no idea. I don't know who sent this."

I contemplate calling the cops, but there isn't much left of the box. Most of it burned, including the note. Only a pile of charred cardboard remains. No concrete clues that will lead to anything. Besides, I doubt SJPD will have time for this given how resource-constrained they have been lately. It's not like anyone was injured in this incident.

I pick up the debris and toss it in the trash after ensuring there's no flame and it won't be a fire hazard. We spend the next couple of hours cleaning ourselves and the living room. Scrubbing out the paint isn't easy.

The explosion has rattled us all, and the house is quiet for the rest of the day. Heather walks around grim-lipped. My ray of sunshine, Joyce, is subdued. It makes my heart ache.

I mull over the incident, trying to make sense of it. *Who would want to hurt us?* A part of me says I'm overreacting. Perhaps that wasn't the intention. It was a genuine gift that went awry. Another part of me counters that that explanation doesn't add up. This was a calculated attack. That would explain why the box was delivered anonymously. But why would anyone want to harm me? Even if someone did hate me enough to do this, why target my family too? Or did the attacker assume I would be alone when I opened the package?

Following that train of thought, I try to come up with a list of suspects. *Who hates me so much?* There's only one person I can think of who is miffed with me. Rhonda. But I have a hard time believing her hatred could be this intense. And just when I think there's no one else to consider, another name pops up, and it makes me sick. Heather. Given the affair, there's no doubt that she detests me. This package was another way to get the message across. But I dismiss this option immediately, because she would never involve the children. No, it can't be Heather. I spend some more time thinking it through, but I come up with nothing.

It isn't until late in the evening that I enter my office to catch up on email. One with the subject "Gift" catches my eye. It's a one-liner from Penelope.

> *Did you like my gift?*

My heart is pounding. *How dare she!* That's all I can think as I dash off a furious email. Her response comes quick.

> *I don't understand. I didn't send you any-thing. I don't even have your address.*

Why would she ask about the "gift" and then deny any knowl-edge of it? I fire off another message, providing more details.

> *Oh no! So sorry to hear about that and re-lieved that you are all safe. The world is full of sickos. By gift I meant the five-star review I left for Her Darkest Fears. I loved it.*

I feel like an idiot for jumping to conclusions and getting angry at her. She's just a diehard fan. I owe her an apology. But before I do that, I should verify her claim. For all I know, she could be lying. I open the Amazon page for *Her Darkest Fears*. There are already thousands of reviews, a stark contrast from those early days of my career when it took weeks to get a review and it was easy to spot a new one. Now I have to sift through tons of reviews to find hers. It takes me a few minutes. The user id says *PenH*. Rated five stars.

A thrilling ride!

Daniel Geraldi has a gift. I've read and enjoyed all his books so far, and this one was no different. I devoured it in one sitting, completely immersed in the story. Guys, don't miss this one!

I feel awful for doubting her. So I start typing.

> *I'm sorry. I misunderstood. Hope you can forgive me.*

Her response arrives a couple of minutes later.

> *Don't worry about it. You were upset. It's understandable.*

It's gracious of her to be so forgiving. I tell her so in my next email, hoping my tirade hasn't turned her off me. Her reply doesn't take long.

> *The other day you were asking about my tattoos. Here's one that should cheer you up.*

I open the attachment. It's a picture of a butterfly tattoo. Cleavage again, but a different kind. This tattoo sits above her butt. The filthy thoughts take root in my mind again. I consider stepping away as I'd done last time, but tonight I need this escape. A voice inside eggs me on, reminding me that Heather's also selfish enough to pursue her own escape.

> *Beautiful. Are there more?*

I eagerly wait for her response. She doesn't disappoint.

> *You can't wait, huh? You naughty boy ;) You're in for a treat.*

I grin as I open the attachment. This one's a rose tattoo in the pelvic area. She has offered enough, just short of revealing any naughty bits. I picture her entire body again, filling in this new information, and I imagine us together in bed — every single detail of what I would do to her and what she would do to me. This is cheating, but tonight I don't care.

9

DANIEL

The explosion haunts us even a day later. It's apparent in the way everyone walks around the house looking morose. And it's torture when Heather carries her Amazon package inside in trepidation. I have to remind myself to breathe. The box is clearly marked and labeled, yet she hesitates and her hands tremble when she opens it. The relief on her face is unmistakable when she flips the flaps and nothing happens.

"We need security cameras," she says. I'm thankful she's calm, because we had this same conversation a few months ago and I assured her I would install some soon. At the time a couple of neighbors had complained about missing packages, and she was concerned it could happen to us, too.

"I'll get on it." This time I mean it. If we had cameras we could have checked who left the package. Or we could have avoided the incident altogether since the cameras would be a deterrent.

The mention of cameras reminds me that the O'Donnells have some. Their system should have captured video of our front door. I share my thoughts with Heather and head out.

Eric and Maisie O'Donnell moved in around a year prior along with their precocious three-year-old, Killian. I usually look forward to seeing them, since Maisie's a huge fan of my books. I still remember how her eyes grew wide at our first meeting when she found out who I was. She was gushing. Back then, it was adorable. Now that I think about it, she could be the one who dropped the package with the claim of being my biggest fan, but I don't see that sweet woman playing such a nasty trick.

Noises emanate from inside as I stand before their door and debate whether I should turn back. It sounds like they're preoccupied, but that's not the only reason I'm hesitant to see them. My last meeting with Maisie is weighing on my mind. Something inappropriate happened, and I expect things will be awkward between us because of it.

The camera footage is more important, so I ring the doorbell anyway. Eric opens the door, looking harried. Behind him, in the distance, a red-faced Killian is bawling away. Maisie's talking to him, her voice barely audible above the toddler's shrill tone, but I can't see her. The floor is littered with Cheerios and a plethora of toys, including pieces of the most deadly weapon known to parents — Legos. My feet instinctively hurt when I remember all those times I stepped on the pieces when the kids were little.

I'm relieved that Eric opened the door, not Maisie. If I'm lucky I'll be able to avoid her.

"Sorry, we're not having a great day here." He musters an apologetic smile.

"Oh. I can come back later."

"No, no, come on in. What's up?"

I step inside and tell him what happened.

His eyes widen in alarm. "That's awful! How can I help?"

"Your security cameras catch our front door, right?"

"Yes, the one in the front does."

"Do you mind if we check the videos? It might have captured whoever dropped the package."

"Sure. Let me get my laptop."

I take a seat in Eric's office, trying to block out the sounds of Killian's tantrum, thankful I don't have to suffer any of that anymore. Somewhere down the road my children will have children of their own. I wonder how Joyce and Jonas will handle such situations. Will they be good parents? I sincerely hope so. A part of me can't wait to become a cool grandpa. I believe grandpas get all the benefits of little ones without having to deal with the negatives like the meltdown little Killian is experiencing.

Eric returns with the laptop after a minute and starts tapping away. Then he frowns.

"Huh. That's weird."

"What happened?"

"It hasn't captured anything for the last two days."

Strange. I think about Maisie again. She would have access to the videos and could have wiped them clean if she was the one who dropped the package. But why would she attack us like that? Could it have something to do with what transpired between us? In my opinion, that would be overkill. Then again, the explosion could have been an accident. I debate whether I should ask her about it, but I eventually chicken out.

"I'm sorry, Daniel. I'll have to check what's going on with it."

"Has it ever done this before?"

"Not that we've noticed. But then, we rarely need to review the videos given how safe this neighborhood is." He pauses, then adds in a softer voice, "Maisie's brother — he's the one who recommended this system. He considers himself to be pretty tech-savvy. Honestly, I disagree." He breaks into a grin. "But don't tell her I said that."

I chuckle. "Don't worry. My lips are sealed."

At least now I know which product to avoid when I'm purchasing cameras for our home.

"Thanks, Eric," I say as I stand up to leave.

Disappointed, I depart. As I cross the street, I consider another option. What if Maisie had nothing to do with the attack? What if it was Eric? Perhaps he found out what transpired between her and me, and this is his way of lashing out. But in either case, whether it was Eric or Maisie, there's no reason to hurt Heather or my kids. Their beef would only be against me. It's quite likely the O'Donnells don't have anything to do with it. Or maybe they do, but they didn't expect me to open the package with the family gathered around. I'm just worried that this might not be a lone incident. It could be the first of many more to come.

"I'm sorry, Dad," Jonas says, once I'm back home.

"What for?" I can't think of anything he needs to apologize for.

"For cussing yesterday. I know you don't like it."

This is another reason why I love my boy. He listens to me and understands me. He cares. He's responsible, unlike a lot of teenagers I know. I remember the time when he was six. We were at the store for some groceries. As usual, he was excited to be there, looking up at me with those adoring puppy eyes every few minutes. A woman remarked that I should enjoy that time and adulation, since "they don't give a damn once they grow up." Well, was she wrong. It's all in how well you raise them. Back then I had a vision of the man he would grow up to be, the man I hoped he would become, and I'm proud to see he's there. It wasn't always easy, though. He developed quite a temper sometime between the toddler phase and his teenage years. It took a lot of patience and guidance on our part to help him deal with his emotions. It's so satisfying to see our hard work pay off.

Everyone in the family knows I detest swear words, but they don't know why. I haven't told anyone, not even Heather. I don't know if I'm ashamed about it, or I don't want to burden them with my woes, but I just haven't been able to discuss it. They all comply and try to talk clean, though I've noticed a smirk on Heather's face every time one of the children accidentally utters a cuss word. I'm not sure why. Someday I'll ask her about it.

The fact is, my father had a drinking problem. He was a reasonable man when he was sober, but a monster once he had one too many. He swore, he hit my mother, whacked me. She tolerated it for years, because in her mind he was still a fine person. Flawed, but decent, is how she put it. That stuck with me. Though foul language is cheap and people use it like normal words, I associate cussing with his deplorable behavior and the trauma we endured because of it.

"That's so responsible of you to step up and apologize. I'm just relieved everyone's safe," I reply.

"Any idea who sent the package?"

"No, not yet. But I hope to find out soon." That's all I can say, and my heart sinks, because there's a flicker of fear in his face before he turns to leave. I've failed my family if I can't keep them safe, can't make them feel secure.

Later that evening I spend some time researching security cameras and order a couple that I like. They'll be here in a week. Heather's delighted to hear about it.

"Finally," she says.

"I told you I'd do it. You didn't have to keep reminding me every three months," I reply with a cheeky grin.

She titters. We kiss. We go to bed, secure in each other's arms, and for a while I force myself to forget that she has a beau.

10

DANIEL

"Can you take Joyce to soccer practice today?" Heather asks. She looks out of sorts, her hair a mess and her eyes puffy. Effects of a lovers' tiff, perhaps? The possibility makes my heart leap with joy. On the other hand, this could be trauma from the package incident, and the thought crushes me.

I'd planned to work on my novel today — a key scene's been camping in my head, ready to go. It's the one where my MC, Fiona, finds her sister dead. This scene kicks off the meat of the story. But I can accommodate Heather here.

"Sure. You doing okay?"

She nods. "Just have a headache, that's all."

Her pain makes me feel guilty. After learning of the affair, I'd resolved to spend more time with her — to be more attentive to her, but I've done none of that. If I really want her to remain in my life, I must step up my game or I risk losing her forever. There's still some time before the practice, so I hand her a glass of water along with a Tylenol. As she gulps it down, I massage her shoulders.

"Mmm ... that feels divine," she says, as if in a trance.

I spend the next twenty minutes continuing the massage, adding in a backrub, a foot massage and topping it up with some work on her temple to ease the headache. She's looking much better by the time I settle into the driver's seat of our Honda Odyssey, with Joyce by my side.

"Riddle me this. Why did the soccer team in Boston lose most of their games?" I ask Joyce as we turn out of our street. A father-daughter car ride isn't complete without a Dad joke.

"Daaaad ..." And a Dad joke attempt isn't complete without a mock protest.

"Come on, Joyce, humor me."

"Does it have anything to do with Boston cream pie?"

"No."

"The Boston Tea Party, then?"

"Nope."

"Okay. I give up."

"Come on, give it a shot."

"Dad, I got nothing."

"Alright, here it comes — because they were wearing red socks." Silence.

"Get it?" I ask in disappointment. While I didn't expect guffaws, I'd expected some reaction. She's deep in thought, trying to figure it out, so I give her some time. And then the light bulb goes on.

"That's, like, the lamest one, Dad," she says, rolling her eyes before turning to me. "But I give you props for mixing soccer with baseball."

She has a faint smile on her face, so I know she secretly enjoyed the joke, and that makes it worth the effort. *Thank you, Boston Red Sox!*

It's a couple of minutes before she speaks again.

"Dad, did you find out anything about the package?"

The quiver in her voice makes my heart ache, the light mood from minutes ago a distant memory. It's agonizing that my daughter had to endure that nerve-wracking experience. The incident still has me spooked too. I choose my words carefully to calm her fears.

"Not yet. But don't worry about it. Probably someone playing a practical joke."

"I ... I didn't find it funny."

"I know. Neither did I. Everyone has different notions of what's funny. The important thing is, we're all okay. It wasn't intended to harm anyone."

Not quite how I wanted to handle it. You would think I'd be better with words considering I'm a professional writer. Heather would have known exactly what to say in this situation. Hopefully my effort did something to calm Joyce's fears.

The rest of the ride passes in silence. I'd originally planned to drop her off and return home, but after our grim talk I decide to stay and watch. The session is only an hour long, and it's been a while since I've seen her play anyway. Though she doesn't say it, I know she'll be happy that I'm watching. Heather always stays.

We get out of the car and walk up to the field. Some of the other girls and their parents are already there. A tall man in track pants is talking to them, and from the looks of it, he has their attention. He turns when he hears us approach. A glance at his face and I freeze. *This can't be.*

It's the man from the motel. Up close he's even more handsome, and it's clear why Heather's attracted to him. My heart is galloping now, and I have an urge to land a few punches on him, to beat him senseless and mess up his pretty face. I clench my fists, take deep breaths and count to ten, letting the feeling pass.

Something is swirling inside him too, because his half-smile disappears and his expression hardens when he sees me. He knows who I am. But there's more to it than hatred for a rival. There's disgust. I wonder what Heather told him about me that would make it so. I can't think of anything. While I may have neglected her a bit, I've always treated her well.

Now I know why this man — Patrick, if I recall correctly — seemed familiar when I saw him at the motel. I'd met him the last time I drove Joyce to practice. It was his first session as coach. He had just moved from Chicago. This means whatever's been going on between Heather and him isn't more than three months old.

I join the other parents on the sidelines, noting the enamored looks he gets from some of the moms. It's an excruciating hour, which I spend fuming for the most part, except for some bright spots where Joyce dazzles with her dribbling skills. I'm relieved when it's all over and we escape into the comfort of our minivan.

"You did well out there. I'm so proud of you," I say.

"Thanks, Dad," she replies as she swells with pride.

A thought nags me on the drive home. Patrick has no qualms about sleeping with a married woman. Where else do his loose morals lead him? He's a young guy, surrounded by adoring teenage girls. Is he taking advantage of them? Especially Joyce. I know she adores him as a coach, but should I be concerned about anything else? I must calm my fears.

"Joyce, what do you think of this new coach?"

"Coach Patrick? I love him. Everyone does."

"Better than the previous one?"

"Oh yeah, way better. He's so sweet. Always encouraging us to improve, but in a gentle way. And he's really awesome at showing us how to control the ball. The previous coach was mean."

"Has he ever made you feel uncomfortable?"

Joyce frowns. "Uncomfortable? How?"

I hesitate before replying. Heather can probably handle this better, but I fear her relationship with the man will cloud her perspective. I must deal with this myself.

"Has he ... has he ever touched you?"

She wrinkles her nose. "Eww, Dad! Why would you ask that? No way! He would never do that."

The response is a relief. At least my daughter is safe from this guy.

"But Mom's really weird with him."

"What do you mean?"

"She gets all giggly when she's talking to him." Joyce pauses. "But a lot of the moms act like that around him."

I wonder how many other women Patrick is stringing along. How soon before he breaks Heather's heart the way she has broken mine?

11

DANIEL

*S*hattered Lives.

That's all the email from Pen says. It's the title of my eleventh novel, the one that preceded my latest one. I speculate on what she means by that. Is she trying to tell me it's her favorite? Or she finished reading it and wants to discuss it? What if she hated it? There's only one way to find out, so I dash off my reply.

> *???*

The suspense kills me as I wait, fearing the worst. Her response arrives a few minutes later.

> *Brutal stuff. Did you really have to write about suicide, especially with all those details?*

This isn't what I expected. One of the key characters in that story takes her own life. I described her issues in detail and explained how she ended things with an overdose of fentanyl. I didn't take it lightly. It was a critical part of the plot, and I conducted extensive research to ensure I got things right and didn't come across as insensitive. There's even a trigger warning prominently included in the blurb as well as at the beginning of the book. Maybe Pen missed it. Maybe she thought she could handle it. I try to explain.

> *I'm sorry if it was triggering. It was important to the story. Did you lose someone close?*

Her reply is back in no time, but she hasn't answered my question.

> *The way you explained how she did it — it doesn't leave anything to the imagination. It's like providing a handbook to everyone out there who's struggling and looking for a way out.*

She has a point, but it's not like the same information isn't available online. In fact, there's a lot more on the internet, and much easier to find than wading through a four-hundred-page novel. I don't know how to respond. It's a sensitive situation, and I must choose my words carefully. I'm not in the right frame of mind for that right now. I log off, but it gets me thinking. Pen, like me, seems to have experienced death up close. My experience induced some darkness in me. I'm sure that's the reason I write the stories that I do. I wonder how Pen's experience affected her. Is she, too, engulfed in darkness? A darkness that compels her to do things she shouldn't be doing?

I'm standing by the door in Annie's bathroom. She's in the tub, unmoving, her eyes closed. Tears stream down my face, and I turn to leave before it's too late.

"Daniel."

The disjointed word startles me, and I whirl around to face her. She's standing now, drenched and dripping water, her piercing eyes cutting through my body, giving me the chills. My knees buckle. I drop to the ground, trembling. She floats out of the bathtub and looms over me. There's no beauty in her face anymore. No innocence either. It's just a hideous mass of black and purple. I shut my eyes, fearing the worst, hoping she's gone by the time I open my eyes. But she's still there when I do. She unleashes an ear-shattering scream before swooping down on me.

I shudder awake, sitting up in bed, soaked in sweat. Another nightmare, a more recent companion. As always, Heather's sleeping soundly next to me. I envy how she's so peaceful. But the truth is, I deserve this torture, every bit of it. I consider changing out of my damp clothes, but I'm too drained to move. Defeated, I lie down and close my eyes in a futile attempt to sleep. The memory continues to haunt me. Hopefully, someday, I'll be free of it.

12

DANIEL

I have a meeting with my editor today, and I'm already running late. Not surprising considering how little I slept last night. I scarf down breakfast, wash it down with a mug of coffee, and rush out the door. My pride and joy, my bright red Porsche 718 Boxster, is waiting outside. I pampered myself by purchasing it after the success of my eighth novel. It still rides beautifully and looks just as new as the day I bought it.

Or at least it did until last evening. I freeze when I set my eyes on the car. Alarm surges through me, and I almost lose my meal. The tires are slashed. It's quite an effort, but I stagger over to the other side of the car to check. Same on that side too. After what happened with the package, I'm now convinced someone is out to get me. Fighting a bout of lightheadedness, I turn to check the Odyssey — its tires are slashed too. I look for Jonas's Civic. Thankfully it's intact. It may have lucked out because it's parked on the street and not in our driveway.

I take a deep breath before fear turns to panic. Peering up and down the street, I scan for any suspicious person, anything out of place, but there's nothing. It's not like the perp would have stuck around, anyway. I'm not making it anywhere today, so I call my editor to inform her I have to cancel due to a personal emergency.

Who could have done this? The same devil who delivered the package? If only those cameras had arrived. I would have installed them and probably avoided this incident. Or at least, I would be able to find out who's responsible.

The O'Donnells' house looms in the distance, and I figure it's worth another shot. I jog over and knock. Unlike my previous visit, this time it's quiet inside. Maisie answers. She appears exhausted, but she manages a smile when she sees me. I'm relieved that she has put our last meeting behind her. It's for the better, otherwise this would have been awkward. I smile back, as if that kiss never happened.

"Eric's not home. He had to leave for an early meeting."

"Perhaps you can help me?"

Concern clouds her face. "Is it about that package? Eric told me about it. That must have been awful."

"It was." Now that she has mentioned the package, I figure I might as well ask her about it. "It wasn't you, was it?"

"What do you mean?"

"I mean — did you send it?"

Her face turns red, her jaw tightens, and when she speaks, her voice is raised. "Why on earth would I do that?"

I realize I could have phrased that better. "Sorry. I didn't mean you wanted to hurt us. Perhaps it was a harmless gift but something went wrong with it."

"Why do you think I sent it?"

"It wasn't mailed, so I figured someone who lived close by dropped it off. And it said 'from my biggest fan.' I thought it could be you."

"I can assure you, it wasn't me." Her tone is cold. So much for avoiding awkwardness. This is going downhill real fast. "Anything else on your mind?"

"Yes. Someone slashed our tires last night."

Her jaw drops. "Oh, that's dreadful." Her eyes dart to her minivan parked in the driveway, probably checking if it's intact. Her gaze returns to me. "You aren't suspecting me, are you?"

"No, no, not at all. I just thought, perhaps, we could check the video from your camera in case it caught anything."

"Sure thing. Come on in. Killian is asleep ... finally."

I enter the house, following her into the living room. She takes a seat at the dining table and starts working on the laptop that's sitting there. I settle in next to her and watch. We were about this close the last time too. That's when we kissed. She initiated it, and I responded. It only lasted a couple of seconds before we both realized it was wrong and pulled away. I apologized and left immediately, riddled with guilt about cheating on Heather. But today, I'm guilt-free. Heather's infidelity has liberated me. I can't help admiring Maisie's luscious lips and imagining what it would be like to kiss her again. The fact is, I'd never noticed her beauty before. But now that I've tasted her, I can't get it out of my mind. Just as quickly as the thought enters my head, I shoo it away. It's not fair to Eric. Besides, it doesn't seem like she's interested.

I wonder why I'm attracted to her today. She's attractive, but not my type. The dark hair, sure, but she keeps hers short, not long the way I like it. Her body is lumpy, and she doesn't have any tattoos — not any that I know of, anyway. Perhaps I'm losing my mind after learning of the affair, and this is me acting out. Perhaps somewhere deep down I feel like I need to prove myself because Heather rejected me in favor of someone else — to prove that I can still woo a beautiful woman. Pathetic.

"I think I have something," Maisie says after a couple of minutes, turning the laptop to face me.

I turn my attention to the screen. The timestamp shows the time as 3:09 a.m. A figure walks down my side of the street and turns into my driveway. Then he crouches and starts working on the tires one by one. First the Porsche, then the Odyssey. The video is dark and grainy, and the culprit is wearing a hoodie so it's difficult to tell who it is, or if it's a man or a woman. Not very useful, but at least it confirms what happened and also gives me a time window. He saunters away once the deed is done.

"What are you going to do now?"

"Call the cops, I guess. Can you send me the video?"

"Sure."

"Thanks, Maisie."

I don't know what the cops can do, but it's worth a shot. I bid her farewell and trudge back home to break the bad news to Heather.

13

DANIEL

As expected, Heather does not take the news well. She panics. She whimpers. She clutches her hair so tight I'm worried she'll pull some out. The children are even more concerned. I've never felt so inadequate before. My family is steeped in fear, and I'm unable to do anything about it. Some may consider it an antiquated way of thinking, but it's my job as the man of the house to protect my family and keep them safe. It's my duty, and I'm failing at it — miserably.

Given the state of SJPD resources, I don't expect much from notifying the cops, but I take some pictures of the damage and file a report online anyway. At least the incident will be on the record. The video from Maisie arrives by the time I'm done. Next, I call around to find someone who can come to our home and replace the tires for both cars. It's going to be a challenge going anywhere with our cars out of commission.

Once the appointment is confirmed, I plop on the couch to take a break. The security cameras aren't here yet. With this latest incident, I'm motivated enough to install them as soon as they arrive. If only I'd listened to Heather and bought the cameras when she had first suggested it. Things are getting out of hand. I wonder who's targeting us like this. Unlike the package, where the label indicated it was from a fan — which I doubt it was — there was no sign of any message this time around. If this person wants to spook us, he — or she — is succeeding.

I spend the next few hours in the office, staring at the screen, trying to work on my novel, but I'm too distracted to get anywhere. It's unfortunate, because my previous session was unproductive as well. I browsed online, caught up on news, watched silly videos, searched for romantic anniversary gifts for Heather, and much more — anything but writing. My time would have been better utilized if I'd gone for a walk instead.

Some may call it writer's block, but a lot of times it's fear that holds me back. Fear that what I'll put on the page won't be literary gold. It's true, though — my first drafts are mostly drivel, and it takes several rounds of editing to polish the text and make it shine. But even after all these years of success, I have to remind myself about it and push through those fears to make progress.

By evening both cars have a fresh set of tires, and I've burned a hole in my pocket. One set is expensive enough — replacing two sets together is just nuts. And we'd changed the tires on the Odyssey only a few months ago. What a waste. But that's the least of my problems.

The mood around the house remains somber. It's a lot worse than in the aftermath of the package. By the time we wrap up dinner, I'm exhausted. There's no way I'm writing anything tonight.

I realize I haven't chatted with Pen in a while. Things were heating up between us, but then she went quiet. Then I remember her email about the suicide. Of course, I forgot to reply to her — or rather, chose not to reply. She raised an issue important to her and I ignored it. No wonder she has disappeared.

I dread talking to her, but I need her. Her and Macallan. Grabbing a glass and a bottle of single malt, I head to my office. Once I'm seated, I pour myself a drink, downing half of it in one greedy gulp. As expected, no emails from Pen. I dash off a quick one to her.

> *It's been a while. How've you been? I had an awful day.*

While I wait for her response, I finish my drink and pour another one, promising myself this will be the last one. I browse the handful of pictures Pen sent me earlier, imagining what it would be like to see her in the flesh. I'm almost convinced I won't hear from her, when the notification pops up. My spirits lift.

> *Aww. You poor dear! Want to talk about it?*

I'm relieved that we're back to normal. Hopefully she has put our last discussion behind her. I pour my heart out, typing furiously, telling her everything that happened and how much I've missed her. The reply comes back quick.

> *That's so awful! Sounds like you need a hug.*

> *I sure do!*

Nervous, I bounce my knee as I wait for her response. The glass is empty. I debate whether I should refill it, but better sense prevails and I don't. In spite of all that transpired today, I'm excited. Pen's got me excited. Guilt threatens to ruin my mood, reminding me that Heather needs me. She was in a dreadful state today, much worse than me. It's not often that I see her looking so pale and distressed. Like any other caring husband, I should be with her in bed, comforting her with warm cuddles, instead of sitting here having an emotional affair with another woman. But then Patrick's mug appears before me and I remember why I'm ignoring my wife. If she craves emotional support she's free to run into his arms.

> *Want to meet? I can give you all the hugs you need ;)*

Pen's latest email warms my heart. I'd have to be crazy to turn down her offer.

> *When? Where? Can we talk now?*

Typing out emails and waiting for a response is getting frustrating. I want to pick up the phone and talk to her. Hear her voice. Make her laugh. Hear her breathe. I want to speak sweet nothings into her ear.

> *You mean talk on the phone? Nah, let's stick to email. I'm kinda enjoying this quaint way of communicating. And it will make it that much more special when I hear your voice in person again.*

She has a point. Besides, it's safer this way. It would be a disaster if Heather stumbled onto anything about Pen on my phone, even if she doesn't have the right to challenge me after what she has done.

So, when and where?

My heart is racing in anticipation. Her response is almost instantaneous.

Pen: How about tonight? In an hour? At Rancho San Antonio?

Me: Won't it be closed at this time?

Pen: And that's why it will be fun to sneak in :) and we will have the place to ourselves. Complete privacy. No one to disturb us ;)

The excitement is building. I don't think I've felt this way since those early dates with Heather. On the one hand, Pen's plan is tempting, but it disturbs me. I'm one to follow rules, always worried about violating any regulations. Parks close at night for a reason, especially Rancho. Besides, I've had a couple of drinks and I'm not sure if I'm in a state to drive.

Me: What about the mountain lions?

Pen: Sheesh! You are such a party pooper! Mountain lions are a problem there even during the day. People still go, right?

I consider the ultimatum. This might be my only chance to meet her, to see her in the flesh. She might lose interest if I chicken out now. I cave, not wanting to miss this opportunity to spend time with her. I can already picture her standing before me, can almost taste her lips, feel the curve of her body with my hands as desire soars inside me. It's high time I get what I want.

We finalize the time and the exact spot within the park where we will rendezvous. Grabbing the keys, I'm headed towards the front door when Heather comes downstairs. *Busted!* Whatever excitement I'd been feeling evaporates and is replaced by a mixture of guilt and nerves.

"You going somewhere?"

"Just need some fresh air," I reply, trying to sound casual.

"I could do with some of that. Mind if I join you?"

Damn! Talk about bad timing.

"Umm ... I'd rather go alone. I just need some time to decompress."

She gives me an odd look and nods like she understands, but I know she's skeptical. A voice inside me urges me to bail, but it's too late. In spite of this close call, I can't leave Pen hanging this late at night. I exit the house and drive away on my new wheels.

14

DANIEL

It's just past 10 p.m. when I turn onto the road leading to Rancho San Antonio County Park. I've only ever been here during daylight, a time when this delight of nature looks inviting. In the darkness it's spooky, and I'm hesitant to continue. It doesn't help that I'm nervous about entering the park after closing hours. Will I be arrested if I'm caught? I don't know. But I've committed to Pen and I'm excited to meet her, so I soldier on.

My heart is already hammering by the time I reach the gate two minutes later. As expected, it's closed to vehicular traffic, with no other car in sight. Either Pen's not here yet, or she parked somewhere else. I stop on the side of the road and get out, walking around the gate and stumbling towards the rendezvous point. It's cool, and as goosebumps spread across my arms, I wish I'd been smart enough to pick up a jacket. A couple of minutes into my hike I hear a car door close in the distance. It's probably Pen. I turn to look, but it's too dark to make out anything. I continue walking.

It takes me ten minutes to reach the spot. There's no one. I hate to admit it, but I'm scared. I should have stopped at one drink, because my woozy head is making things worse. All kinds of intimidating shapes form in the darkness around me, and a few times I think I see a mountain lion, but I realize it's just my eyes playing tricks. The gentle rustle of the leaves doesn't help, because it gives the impression that someone is approaching.

The hint of danger awakens my senses. The creative inside me spies ideas. I must write a scene with Fiona in this kind of situation. Perhaps she's stumbling through a forest late at night, all alone. She might be in peril, she's not sure, but her focus is on the task at hand. It could be the highlight of the novel if I develop it further. The thought pleases me for a while, before I return to my disappointing reality.

Still no sign of Pen. *Did she bail on me?* It would suck if she did, considering I stuck to my commitment in spite of the encounter with Heather. This is where it would have been helpful to have Pen's phone number. At least I could have called her to check if she's on her way. Now I wish I'd set up email on my phone like Jonas suggested. It's possible Pen has emailed me with a change of plans, but there's no way for me to know.

Before I can figure out my next move, I hear movement behind me — more than the gentle rustle of leaves or the whistling wind — a twig snaps, leaves crunch. Pen, hopefully.

I don't get a chance to turn around and greet her, though, because something hard connects with the back of my head. The pain is unbearable, and I stagger for a second before collapsing to my knees. My upper body hits the ground soon after. My head hurts, my brain's foggy, and I'm terrified. As I writhe in agony, I notice someone standing over me, holding something. It's too dark to tell who it is, but the attacker is poised to strike again. I should fight back, but my body isn't interested in combat mode. So I cover my head and wait for the next blow to fall, fearing I'll never see my family again.

15

DANIEL

My head is throbbing when I awake. My mouth reeks of alcohol and stale breath. The sun is shining bright, and it takes me a while to figure out where I am. My watch says it's 7:12 a.m. In the distance the early hikers and runners are going about their business. No one seems to have noticed me yet. I struggle to get on my knees, my head swimming as I do so. Once I've stabilized, I stand up. It's a few moments before I'm comfortable enough to walk. The sun hurts my eyes. I touch the back of my head and detect a concerning bump. It brings back traumatic memories of last night. Brutal. I pinch my arm, surprised I'm still alive.

Twenty minutes later I'm at the spot where I parked. My car is gone. Towed, I guess. I consider calling Heather, but I'm not sure how I would explain what I'm doing here or what happened to me. It's the same reason I can't report this incident to the cops. Like pretty much everything else that has transpired between Pen and me, this incident will remain our secret.

I call an Uber. In a way, I'm thankful I don't have to drive in my condition. But I'm not looking forward to the effort involved in retrieving my car. My ride takes forever to arrive, but when it finally does, it's a sight for sore eyes. I get in and shut my eyes, trying to take my mind off the searing pain. Thankfully, the driver is not one of the chatty ones, allowing me to enjoy the peace and quiet that I need.

Soon I'm at the impound lot. While I wait for my turn, I realize my throat is parched. It's probably been this way all morning, but I didn't notice due to the splitting headache. I'll just have to ride this out. Some excruciating minutes and a hefty fine later, I'm reunited with my Boxster. The half-empty bottle of water in the center console doesn't do much to quench my thirst, but it's better than nothing. Then I'm on my way home, battling traffic.

Jonas's car is nowhere to be seen when I get there. He probably had an early start today. Heather and Joyce are in the kitchen, yakking away. They turn to me, concern clouding their faces.

"Dad, where were you?"

"Just went for a hike."

"In jeans?" Joyce is giving me that incredulous look, the teenage kind that is reserved for the uncool things I do.

"Yes."

"Are you okay? You look awful."

"I'm fine, sweetie."

I turn to Heather. She's calm, which is surprising. I'm sure she must have noticed that I'm wearing the same clothes I went out in last night. That I never came to bed. *What's going on in her head?* If I'm lucky, I'll hear about it later. And if I don't, it probably means she doesn't care about me anymore. That there's no turning back from Patrick now. That possibility hurts me way more than the blow I took last night.

After downing a couple of glasses of water, I grab some ice from the fridge and put it in a Ziplock bag. Then I go to the living room to place it on the back of my head. Too many questions if I do that in the kitchen. While I soothe my head, I consider who could have attacked me. It had to be Pen. Who else would have been there at that hour, anyway? She's the one who invited me. There's a reason she picked that time and location. I was gullible enough to accept. After the package and the tires, I should have had my guard up. Instead, I presented myself on a platter. To think I was worried about mountain lions, completely missing the danger posed by this vixen. It's a relief she didn't kill me.

Once my head's a little better, I amble to the office to check my email. There's one from Pen. I open it, curious about what she has to say about her absence last night. Or at least, her apparent absence.

> *Sorry I couldn't make it last night! Car broke down. Hope you didn't wait long.*

For a moment I'm inclined to believe her. It could happen to anyone. But it's too suspicious. It can't be a coincidence that she sent me the email about the gift the same day I received the package, and now I got bonked on the head when I showed up for a tryst with her. She's lying. That's what my instinct tells me, though I don't know how to link her to the slashed tires. Perhaps I missed a message somewhere. *What's her motive?*

I debate whether to tell her about the attack and decide not to. I don't even bother replying. Instead, I trudge upstairs and hop in the shower. My head still hurts, but the hot water refreshes me, and for a short while I feel better. However, the uneasiness returns once I step out. By the time I dry myself off I can't resist the bed, drifting into deep sleep within seconds.

I walk down the cobbled streets of Paris, just like Gil did in Midnight in Paris. *Soon I'm at a café, sitting opposite Ernest Hemingway, requesting him to read my novel. My mind is a roller coaster of emotions as he rejects me first, then says he can get Gertrude Stein to read it, and eventually, I lose him.*

Once I'm done there, I follow Kaufman's journey through all-too-familiar writer's block in the quirky Adaptation. *Then I'm watching James Caan in* Misery *as he celebrates his typed-up manuscript, taking me back to those early days of my career when I pecked away at my Underwood Champion. There was something satisfying about seeing the pages pile up, a pleasure that can't be derived from working on a computer.*

Caan is chained in bed now, Kathy Bates standing at the foot, sledgehammer in hand. An instant later I realize I'm the one in shackles, and I glance up, horrified to see it's Pen, not Bates who's standing bedside, her eyes oozing menace. She raises the hammer and brings it down hard on my leg.

I wake up with a start. I'm quite sure I screamed, too. Yes, I definitely did, because Heather rushes into the room, her face a picture of concern.

"Are you okay?" she asks as she sits beside me and strokes my back in that gentle way that only she can. I have an urge to lay my head in her lap and go back to sleep while she caresses my head.

"I guess."

"Bad dream?"

I take a moment to consider the question, shuddering when I recall what frightened me. A new nightmare. Dreams about movies featuring writers are a frequent occurrence. It's comforting to see glimpses of myself in the characters, to observe that my insecurities as a writer are not unique. But this is the first time a dream like that has taken such a dark turn. No doubt it's a direct consequence of my misguided adventure last night. I can't share this with Heather.

"Yes." It's all I can muster in response to her question.

"Want to talk about it?"

I shake my head. She strokes my hair, mercifully avoiding the spot where I was hit. A soft kiss lands on my lips. First her touch and now this. It helps with my pounding head. I'll be okay, I tell myself as I ease out of bed. I'll be okay as long as Heather's by my side. But not for long, unless I do something about Pen.

16

DANIEL

How do I handle Pen?

That's the burning question. If she's behind all these incidents, I must find her and shut her down. But how? I don't know where she lives, and I don't have her phone number. All I have is her name and email address. The name is a dead-end. I've spent hours searching online with different combinations, following several leads that led nowhere. I'm convinced she gave me a fake name. The email address is my only option, but I have no idea how to trace the owner. I don't expect much from the cops, considering their non-existent response to my report on the tire-slashing incident. I could ask Jonas, since he's a whiz at all this technical mumbo jumbo, but I don't want to suck him into this nonsense. He, like the rest of the family, has already had to deal with enough. So what do I do?

Then I realize there is one person who might be able to help me. Venky. His full name's Venkatraman, with an even longer last name which I won't attempt because I butcher it every time I try. He's a techie — a smart one — and he lives a couple of houses down the street. I've consulted him before on technical details for some of my novels.

"Where did you go last night, Dad?" Jonas has entered the living room with a bowl of popcorn. He offers me some and I grab a handful.

"Just went for a drive. I needed to clear my head."

"And where did Mom go?"

My hand stops in mid-air, still holding the popcorn, my salivating mouth open in anticipation.

"Heather went out last night?"

"Yes. Right after you left."

I raise my eyebrow. "You're keeping tabs on everyone, Sherlock?"

He shrugs. "Can't help it. You forget my room faces the driveway. I can hear pretty much everything when it comes to our cars. Doors opening and closing. The engine revving. Gotta be sure no one's trying to steal 'em. You know how property crimes are shooting up around here. I just wish I'd heard the jackass who slashed our tires."

I shake my head. "I have no idea where she went."

As I dunk the rest of the popcorn from my hand into my mouth and chew, I mull over this new information. *Where did Heather go?* My first thought is that it's nothing to worry about — she needed an escape, too, when she asked to come with me, and she probably went for a solo drive. But then darker thoughts encroach. What if she left for a tryst with Patrick? Or worse — did she follow me to Rancho? Could she have ...

No. I arrest the thought in place. Heather may have cheated on me, but she would never harm me. This is the same woman who delights me with soft kisses, who comforts me with her caress when I'm down. She could not have been the one who whacked me senseless. I stand up before more such baseless theories consume me.

"I'm going over to Venky's," I say and head over.

It's a short walk, but it's refreshing. Venky's beaming when he opens the door. It's been weeks since we last met. We exchange a firm handshake and I enter. The house smells pleasant, as it always does.

"So, what will it be, bud? Coffee or beer?" he asks.

Venky makes the most amazing coffee. It's Indian filter coffee, he has told me, popularly referred to as *filter kaapi*. But today I need beer.

"Got any Blue Moon?"

"Always well-stocked, my friend."

He opens the fridge and returns with two cold ones. We clink bottles before taking ample gulps of the nectar.

"I'm so happy to see you," he says. "Piya and the kids are in India. It's been too quiet in here."

"Always a pleasure to see you too, Venky." I look around. "How the heck do you keep the place so clean with Piya gone? My house would be a mess without Heather."

Venky shrugs. "What can I say, I'm a neat freak. And honestly, the kids are responsible for ninety percent of the mess."

"True that," I reply as we burst into laughter.

We chat about this and that, catching up on recent events before I bring up the reason for my visit.

"So you want to trace this person's location from emails you've received?"

"Yes."

"May I know who's this person?"

I hesitate.

"Is everything okay, Daniel?" he asks, concern writ on his face.

"Not really." I give him the whole story, leaving out the bit about Pen and me flirting. He doesn't need to know that.

"Wow. That sounds crazy." He pauses, taking a swig of his beer. "Did you try the cops?"

I shake my head. "They're too understaffed to pursue this. They have more important things to take care of."

"You bet. The local news is so depressing these days. Homicide here, burglary there. Not to mention the constant threat of wildfires."

I nod. "So, is there any way I can trace her?"

"It can certainly be done. You see, every email has details about where it came from and how it got from the sender's device to yours. We just have to get the sender's IP address and map that to a geographical location. That's assuming, of course, this woman is not savvy enough to use a VPN or proxy to hide her true location."

My hopes soar. "Interesting. And how do we get this mapping?"

"That's where things get tricky. We're not cops so we can't just subpoena an ISP for those details. There are other ways of getting the information, but those are illegal and could get us in trouble."

My hopes sink just as quickly. "So we can't get her location without help from SJPD?"

"No. What I'm saying is, I know someone who can help, but his services don't come cheap."

"I'm in, as long as I don't have to sell the house to afford this guy."

Venky chuckles. "He's not *that* expensive. Maybe you just have to hold off on that trip to Bora Bora for a while."

Heather and I have our twenty-first anniversary coming up, and we have a relaxing jaunt to the South Pacific island planned. If the pictures are anything to go by, it's a breathtaking place, and I would hate to miss out on this vacation. Heather will definitely throw a fit if we don't go. But what must be done must be done. In any case, I'm sure she'll be thinking about Patrick while she's there.

"It will be worth it if this guy can get me her location."

Venky grabs a Post-it and scribbles something on it. "This is how you contact him. Destroy this as soon as you're done. And if shit hits the fan and someone asks how you learned of him, you didn't hear it from me."

"Got it. Thanks, Venky. I owe you one."

"No problem, Daniel. You take care of yourself."

I pocket the note, and we continue chitchatting for a while as we down some more beers. By the time I leave the house I'm buzzed and hopeful, confident that I can put an end to all the nonsense once I find Pen.

❖

Later that night I draft an email to the address on the Post-it. Venky didn't give me a name — only the address. It's funny how it's so easy to contact this hacker. I'd thought I would have to navigate the dark web and use some convoluted way to connect with him. I keep the message brief, only stating what I need.

The response arrives within minutes. *It will cost you five thousand dollars*, it says. That's not too bad. Bora Bora's still on, baby. I reply, confirming I'm good for it, and he gives me an account number to which I should wire the funds before he begins the job. This surprises me again, because I was sure he would request payment in Bitcoin or some other cryptocurrency.

I hesitate. I don't know who I'm talking to. What if this person disappears with my money? But Venky's the one who provided the referral, and I trust Venky. So I proceed. Once the payment is complete, the hacker requests the details, which I provide.

Three hours later he shares the information I need. Way sooner than I expected. Pen's been using the computers at the Martin Luther King, Jr. Library in Sacramento. Another surprise. I'd expected a location closer to home. I wonder what she's doing out there. Only one way to find out. I'm going to Sacramento.

17

DANIEL

"You're going where?" Heather asks, as if I'm headed to the South Pole. She hates Sacramento. It's too much of a small town for her, with nothing much to do. In my opinion it can be a charming place and worth the occasional visit, though I don't think I could live there. Besides, it deserves some respect as the state capital.

"You heard it right the first time. I'm going to Sac."

"So your next novel's set in Sac? Why?"

"It's not based there. One of the key characters is from there. I need to do some research for her backstory."

Heather's brow is arched, face stern. It's the same expression she has when she's calling the kids on their BS. For a moment I'm worried she'll figure out I'm up to no good.

"When will you be back?"

"A couple of days, tops." I'm hoping I can find Pen today so that I can return early, but it's possible she doesn't visit the library every day.

"Next time write a character from Tahoe or Yosemite. Then I can join you, and we can make a fun vacation of it."

I smile. "You know I won't get any research done if you're there with me. I won't be able to keep my hands off you."

It's the truth. In spite of everything that has happened, I'm still attracted to her. Sure, every time we kiss, I gag with the realization that Patrick's lips venture this same way. And when I make love to her, I'm reminded that his hands roam her body too. But I try to block it all out because I want this marriage to work. I'm too weak to envision a life without her.

It's her turn to smile. "I'll miss you," she says.

I walk over to her and take her in my arms. She presses her soft lips to mine. We kiss as I stroke her back to comfort her. Until recently I would have been delighted to accept this expression of affection from her, but these days it's disturbing. It occurs to me that this could all be an act, and she's thinking of Patrick right now — excited that she'll be able to spend some more time with her lover over the next few days. The thought makes me sick. I separate myself from Heather and go upstairs to pack, exhausted by the conflicting emotions she raises inside me.

Soon I'm headed out the door and en route to Sacramento. Along the way I entertain myself with music — everything from Bryan Adams to Duran Duran to the Bee Gees. There's traffic in patches, and it takes me three hours to reach the library. I park and get out of the car, eager to lay eyes on Pen. Once inside the building, I head over to the aisle of computers, but she's nowhere to be found. I roam the aisles of books, just in case she's taking a break and browsing. But she's not there either. I'll have to wait, hoping that she'll be in later.

I grab a book and settle into one of the chairs, a location from which I have a clear view of the computer area. I try to read, but I can't concentrate, my eyes straying from the page every time I sense movement in front of me. Hours pass and it's closing time. Still no sign of her.

Disappointed, I exit the library. Maybe she'll be here tomorrow. Or, perhaps, she has no reason to visit the library unless she's going to send me an email? Which means I'll have to bait her.

I drive off in my car and find a motel to spend the night, realizing I shouldn't have been so optimistic. Once in my room, I open my laptop and fire off a message to Pen.

Hello, stranger. Haven't heard from you in a long time. Everything ok?

Fingers crossed that this will do the trick. There's a chance I'm facing a chicken-and-egg problem — will she be able to read my note without access to the library computers? I'm betting she does have email access at home, but she's been careful not to send anything from there.

I call Heather and let her know I'll be staying the night. She sounds dejected. Once again, I can't decide how I feel about that. Is she genuinely disappointed, or is she delighted at the thought of more time with Patrick? And where is she now? At home, or nestled in the arms of Casanova?

Blocking out the thoughts before they drive me crazy, I head out to grab dinner at a diner across the street. A greasy, satisfying meal later, I'm back in my room. At first, I'm disappointed when there's no response from Pen. But it gives me hope that she will visit the library tomorrow to respond. I put the laptop away and lie down. For a change, sleep comes easy.

I awake early the next morning and return to the diner for yet another heart-attack-inducing feast. With breakfast out of the way, I eagerly head to the library. Today's the day I'll lay eyes on Pen — I can feel it. When I get there, I scan the computer section again. No luck. I grab another book and sit on the same chair as yesterday. It's the same routine — I'm stuck at the first page, since my mind is elsewhere.

Two hours go by, but no sign of Pen. I'm beginning to lose hope. What if the hacker gave me the wrong information? Desperate for fresh air, I step outside the building. It's hot, and I'm almost tempted to return indoors to air-conditioned comfort when I spot a woman heading towards me. It's her. She's just as radiant as she was the last time I saw her, her curves still enticing. I can't help but feel attracted to her all over again before I remind myself what she's capable of. This woman is dangerous.

It's not until she's close to the entrance that her gaze lands on me. She freezes. It's as if I've knocked the wind out of her, because she looks sickly. I grin and take a step towards her. She panics and races back the way she came.

"Hey! Pen! Wait!" I say, but she doesn't comply.

I chase her, but I can already tell she's too fast for me. The gap between us increases with every passing second. She turns by the park, and I follow. The sun is beating down hard, with no hope for any shade in this wide-open area. There's barely a tree in sight. One minute in, I realize I'm way out of shape, because my quads and my lungs are screaming in a symphony of agony. I keep pushing myself, keeping her in my sight until she turns into a side street. By the time I make the turn, she's nowhere to be seen. I've lost her, and it's clear from the way I'm panting that the chase is over even if I manage to spot her again. Disappointed, I collapse onto a bench to catch my breath. Sweat is pouring out of every pore — it's like I've sprung a leak. I mop whatever I can with my handkerchief. As if that's not enough, my skin's burning. I feel weak, old.

All those years I've watched Rhonda go running religiously four times a week. I can't say I haven't been inspired to exercise, but I've rarely followed through. Not even when she had the nerve to point out that my gut had started showing. If anything, that comment turned me off running. Now I wish I'd taken better care of my body. A fitter me could have nabbed Pen. I resolve to start exercising once I'm back home.

When my breathing returns to normal, I trudge back to the library. It takes forever. There's no way Pen's coming back now that she knows I'm here, but I still stick around for a few hours as I formulate my plan. *Have I blown my only chance to find her?*

When the library closes at 6:00 p.m., I reluctantly exit. I'm in no mood to eat, but I stop at the diner for dinner, scarfing down something tasteless to keep my stomach full. It's late by the time I return to my room. I hop into the shower, feeling a lot better by the time I'm done. A quick call to Heather — more disappointment from her, more speculation in my head — and then I check my email. Surprise!

> *You really scared me, Daniel. Sorry I took off like that.*

After what happened today, I hadn't expected anything from Pen.

> *Me: I don't understand. Why were you scared? I thought you would be happy to see me. A pleasant surprise after our previous missed encounter.*

> *Pen: It's not that I am scared of you. I just didn't expect you there, of all places. I panicked. Sorry.*

> *Me: So can we meet tomorrow? No surprises.*

This flurry of emails is followed by silence. I don't have to be a genius to know that she doesn't want to meet me. She's content to play this game of email ping-pong. It makes sense if she's not really interested in me, and all she wants to do is mess with my life. *But why?* That's the question that nags me. I must find her. And this time, when I do, I'm not letting her go.

After giving it some thought I realize, in the words of my favorite fictional detective, that I'm an imbecile. Pen could not have been sending emails only from the library. If she was, how has she been replying after library hours? It means there's another location, perhaps her home, where I can trace her. Even the messages she sent me today must have come from outside the library, given the timing.

This is promising. I send the latest emails to the hacker and ask him to locate her again. It will cost me another five grand, but I'm so close that it would be a shame to let her slip away.

The next morning I have a response from the hacker. He has traced Pen to a single-family home not far from the library. It makes sense that she visits the branch closest to where she lives. I quickly change and head over. No way she's escaping me this time. My stomach growls as I turn onto her street, reminding me that I haven't eaten anything. I never skip breakfast, so this is a first. This sacrifice better be worth it.

I park the car a couple of houses before hers and watch. It's a beautiful structure, with a well-maintained front yard covered with lush green grass. I'm curious to view the interior. To kill time, I look up the address on Zillow. It's one of those tricks Jonas taught me. It makes me a bit less technologically backward. There's only one picture of the exterior. No interior pictures. The home last sold over thirty years ago. So she's been here a long time, probably her entire life. Or perhaps she's renting?

Finding no other useful info, I exit the site and return to idle waiting. An hour goes by, but there's no sign of Pen. I'd hoped she would step out at some point, and I would be able to confirm that she lives here.

Tired of waiting, I get out of the car and walk towards her front door. The curtains are drawn. I take one last peek at the street before knocking. No response. I knock again. Still nothing. This time I ring the doorbell, wondering why I didn't think of that earlier. Probably because I'm nervous. My palms are sweaty, and I wipe them on my jeans. Another jab at the doorbell. My watch shows it's 9:00 a.m. Pen should be up by now. I can't explain it, but I'm sure she's an early riser. Disappointed, I raise my fist to knock again.

"What do you want?"

It's a relief to receive a response, but it's not what I'd expected at all. The speaker is behind me, not inside the house. And it's a male voice. I turn to face a tall, muscular man standing not more than twenty feet from me. There's something menacing about his tone and demeanor, but that's not what spooks me the most. He's wearing a cop uniform. I sense I'm in trouble.

"I ... I ..." My mouth's dry. I lick my lips to wet them and run my tongue around the inside of my mouth. "I'm here to see Pen."

"Pen?" He raises an eyebrow, clearly not convinced by my reply. "Come here," he says, gesturing with his index finger.

I take a few steps towards him. When I stop, I hear the door opening behind me.

"Is he the one?" he asks, looking past me towards the front door. I turn around to see Pen standing in the doorway. She's staring at me.

"Yes," she replies.

He returns his gaze to me, a hint of a smirk on his face. "You got nothing better to do, harassing decent women around here?"

"That's not what—"

"Don't bullshit me. You and me, we're taking a trip to the station."

My knees tremble. "You're ... you're arresting me?" I manage in a shaky voice.

He nods, turns me around and cuffs me as he reads me my rights. I can't believe this is happening. Perhaps it's all a dream? But I glance at Pen, and she's got a devilish grin on her face. This is for real. She set me up, knowing it was only a matter of time before I would track her down again. As with that night at Rancho, I've fallen into her trap once again. Before I can say anything, she disappears inside her house and slams the door shut.

I spend the night in jail. For a while I'd considered calling Heather and having her bail me out, but how would I explain my situation? On the other hand, how will I explain why I didn't call her like I do every evening? If I rot in this cell any longer, she'll be worried, not knowing where I am. Maybe I should have called her after all.

My thoughts are interrupted by movement outside. The same officer who arrested me is standing there. He unlocks the door and pulls it wide open. The smirk is still plastered on his face, as if he takes pleasure in my suffering.

"You're free to go," he says.

I can't believe my ears. Surely he's messing with me.

"I said, you can leave. You're not under arrest anymore," he repeats when I don't move.

I stand up and float towards the door as if in a trance. I still suspect it's a prank, and he'll slam the door in my face before I can exit. But he doesn't. I step out of the cell, and he places his hand on my shoulder, glaring at me.

"If I ever see you again in Sacramento, if I ever learn you've been within a hundred feet of her, I swear I'll personally skin you alive."

His words send a shiver down my spine. Sure, I'll stay away from Pen, but my concern is — will she stay away from me? I want to explain that I'm not the dangerous one — Pen is. That I'm not the aggressor, and I'm only defending myself and my family from her. But it would be futile, because he's in her corner. I don't dare risk my new-found freedom by saying anything.

We walk down the corridor in silence. Soon I've completed the release formalities and I step out of the building, a free man. My cell's at a measly five percent battery, and it shows several missed calls and texts from Heather. I send her a quick text to tell her I'll be home soon before heading back to the motel to check out. On the drive home all I can think of is the hot shower I'll take when I get there, the warm embrace I'll give Heather, and the soft comfort of my bed as I settle into a deep sleep. I've never missed it all more.

18

ANONYMOUS

I'm a runner. I've always been one since as long as I can remember. Dad used to take us, or rather, force us to run four days a week. At freakin' six in the morning. It was a pain at first, but as I got better, I realized I enjoyed it. The rush of speed, the cool wind against my face. That sensation of strength, and the aftereffects that followed me the rest of the day. I felt fit and so much more energetic.

I'd still whine, though. Dad would try to motivate me, telling me that this was training in case I bumped into a bear at Yosemite someday. At least I'd be able to run for my life. I'd reply insisting that I couldn't outrun a bear, no matter how hard I trained. He would laugh and counter that I didn't have to be faster than the bear — I just had to be faster than whoever else I was with. Mom would roll her eyes, reminding me that it would be selfish, that I should never abandon my friends or family when they're in trouble. Sticking around to help them would be the right thing to do.

What she said made sense, like it always did. Of course, I knew Dad was joking, or at least I thought he was. Anyway, I've seen how running has helped save me in more ways than one, and for that I'll always be grateful to Dad.

19

DANIEL

I awake to a familiar, annoying sound. My mind's still foggy, and I'm unsure whether I'm receiving a call or it's my alarm. Peeking through half-closed eyes, I realize that it's not my phone. Of course it isn't. This is Heather's ringtone.

"Damn junk calls," she mumbles when she sees who's calling and slams her phone back on the nightstand.

She shuts her eyes. I do the same. We're both hoping we can capture sleep again, but, alas, it's not to be. Her phone rings again a few minutes later. She grabs it and sets it to silent mode. That's a relief. The room is quiet for a while, but I'm wide awake now and there's no going back. I hop out of bed. It's 7:30 a.m. Most days I'm already up by this time, but I've been exhausted after recent events. Besides, I was up late last night writing in an attempt to catch up on my novel.

Clearly, Heather can't get much sleep either, because she's out of bed shortly after me. Her phone rings again as soon as she brings it out of silent mode.

"You sure are popular today," I say.

She glares at me as she answers. Within seconds her expression changes to one of disgust and she hangs up.

"Who was that?"

"Some pervert."

We move to the kitchen. I brew the coffee and we sit at the island with our mugs. The kids are still in their rooms. There's a knock at the door just as I'm taking a huge gulp of the nectar. It's frustrating that I can't even drink my morning cuppa in peace. I sigh and walk over to the door, opening it a crack. It's Rhonda. She rarely comes to the house, especially not at this early hour, so I'm curious. Somehow I don't think she's here to share a review of whatever she's been reading.

"What happened to your minivan?" she asks.

Not the tires again. That's the first thought that crosses my mind, and I feel sick, wondering what calamity has struck this time.

"You should check it out," she continues when I don't reply.

Her grave tone doesn't help. I step outside, with Heather right behind me. One glance at the minivan and we both gasp. My stomach rumbles in despair.

"What kind of sick person would do this?" I'm picturing what I would do to the sicko once I find him ... or her.

Heather starts sobbing. I don't blame her. Someone has painted a silhouette of a naked woman in bright red. Next to it are the words "Call me" and Heather's cell phone number.

"This ... this explains the calls," she says, her voice a whisper.

I'm not so sure about that. The van's been in our driveway all this time and it's still early. Not many people could have seen this.

Besides, it's a decent neighborhood and I don't expect the residents would make those profane calls. Something's not adding up.

I rush inside the house, grab a blanket, and return outside. I place it on the van to cover the graffiti, and I put a brick from our front yard on top so that the covering does not fly away. This should work while we figure out what to do next.

"Thanks, Rhonda," I say. "I suppose you didn't see who did this."

She shakes her head. "No idea. I just noticed it when I stepped out for my run."

We return inside the house. Heather collapses on the couch, her sobs getting louder. Unfortunately, the kids are up now, fixing breakfast in the kitchen. I was hoping we would be able to spare them this distress. They join us when they hear their mother crying.

"Mom, what happened?" Joyce asks, her face knitted with concern. Jonas carries the same anxious expression.

For a second I debate whether I should tell them the truth. With everything that has gone wrong recently, I don't want to burden them with one more worry. But this will be difficult to hide. So I tell them. Joyce gasps, not unlike the way Heather and I reacted a few minutes ago. Jonas's face reddens, his jaw and fists clenched. I've never seen him so angry.

"Who's doing all this, Dad?"

I shake my head. "I wish I knew."

He storms out. I turn my attention back to Heather, and as I try to comfort her, my mind wanders to Rhonda. Is it possible she's behind all these incidents? It's quite convenient that she's the one who found the graffiti first. Given that she lives so close to us, it would be so easy for her to walk up to our door or driveway and do something nasty. She hated my guts after the Bruno incident — even though she seems to have mellowed a bit, if I consider the fact that she's been reading my books. But then, it wouldn't make sense for her to attack the rest of my family. Heather and the kids adore dogs, Bruno in particular. No, I doubt Rhonda has anything to do with it.

Could it be Pen again? As if getting me arrested wasn't enough. If anything, that win must have emboldened her. Yes, it's possible this is Pen's work. I don't know what I can do about it though, considering my failed Sac trip.

"We need to fix it. I'll find a body shop." That's all I can muster, not sure how else to console Heather.

Jonas returns. "The other cars are okay," he reports.

"Well, that's a relief," I say.

Heather's phone rings again.

"You should change your number right away," I suggest. She nods.

While Heather calls our carrier to change her number, I search for body shops. Twenty minutes later I've found one close to home that has some room for a paint job. The blanket's not going to cut it on the way there. Besides, I don't want the employees at the shop getting any nasty ideas. I grab a brush and a can of paint from the garage — it's left over from when Joyce painted her room. I paint over the graffiti with it. This should be good enough for the ride.

Satisfied with my work, I get in the van to drive it to the body shop. I'm worried. The stress of the situation is giving me a piercing headache. Whoever's doing all this is crazy. And dangerous. I wonder how else this person could harm us. In hindsight, that incident with the package of exploding paint seems so innocuous. But that's where all this started. It was a warning sign of what was to come.

I turn onto the main street. My heart sinks when I see the bus stop near the first intersection. There's graffiti on the shelter — same as what's on our van. So that's where those perverts got her number. How many other places did this brute do this? How exposed are we? I stop on the side of the road, pick up the box of tissues from the center console, and a bottle of water from the back of the van, and I walk over to the shelter. I wet the tissues and try to scrub off Heather's number. It's quite an effort, but soon I've gotten most of it off — enough to keep her number safe while she works on getting it changed.

I return to the van and scout the neighboring streets for more signs of graffiti, but I find nothing. Then I drive down the main street in the direction opposite to the body shop, but it's clean, too. Satisfied, I turn around and head towards the body shop.

Once I get there I explain that I need the entire section painted over. Of course, the guy tells me he'll have to paint a lot more area to make it look even. My eyes pop out of their sockets when I hear the estimate, but what must be done must be done. Thankfully, we can afford this. I complete the paperwork, drop off the car and the key, and take an Uber back.

Heather's looking much better when I get home. The color's back in her cheeks, and the frown's gone, but her eyes still tell the story of the morning's events. I'll take any improvement over nothing at all.

She has initiated the number change. Joyce still looks nervous, so I talk to her for a bit to calm her fears. Jonas seems to have recovered. I'm relieved that things are under control, but I'm furious at myself again for procrastinating on the cameras. It's about time I get some clues about who is wreaking havoc on our lives. While Pen still tops the list of suspects, I need definitive proof.

I trek over to the O'Donnells' once again. Eric is glad to assist once he gets over the initial shock about what happened. But his camera was on the fritz again, and there are no recordings from last night. I thank him, but suspicion looms in the recesses of my mind. Suspicion that Eric and Maisie might be behind all this. It's strange that the camera hasn't worked during most of the incidents. If it's really so glitchy, why haven't they replaced the system yet? There's a reason they installed it in the first place, so if it's not meeting their needs, why don't they do something about it?

20

DANIEL

It's 6:30 in the morning and I'm in the kitchen brewing my coffee, fretting over the latest incident, when Jonas enters.

"You're up early," I say, concerned that he's stressed about it too. Since it's not a school day, I expected him to sleep in and make the most of the holiday.

"Wanna join me for a hike?"

That's a relief. He has probably gotten over it already. I should have figured. Hiking's the one thing that will pull him out of bed at this hour. I'd planned to work on my novel this morning, but the offer is tempting. This might be one of the last opportunities to spend quality time with my boy before he flies off to college. Over the years we've had some amazing hikes together. Those treks helped us bond, and I'll miss that once he's gone.

"Sure. Where do you want to go?"

"Rancho?"

It's like a jolt to my system. After I got whacked the other night, Rancho San Antonio Park is forever tainted in my mind. I can't handle going there again. Ever. It's too traumatic. My face must have scrunched up in a frown, because Jonas gets the hint without my saying a word.

"Mission Peak, then?" he asks.

I wrinkle my nose. It used to be a terrific place to hike until it got overrun with the crowds. Now parking is a pain, and there are too many people on the trail. It's turned into a Bay Area cliché, with every second person posting a picture of themselves at the summit, clinging to the pole. I'm guessing that's what provoked someone to steal the pole recently.

"How about Uvas Canyon?" I suggest. We've hiked there before. Not only is it my preferred hiking spot, it gives me an excuse to visit BookSmart, one of my favorite indie bookstores. I'll probably end up buying a half-dozen new paperbacks to add to my never-ending TBR pile.

Jonas often ribs me about my preference for physical books. He consumes everything on his Kindle and considers this as another indication that I'm still stuck in the Dark Ages. I'll admit I am old-school in a lot of areas. If Netflix hadn't stopped their DVD service, I would still be renting DVDs by mail instead of wading into the world of streaming. Until recently I was even typing up manuscripts on my Underwood Champion. I only transitioned to writing on my laptop after my agent and publisher insisted.

Jonas gives me the thumbs-up. He likes Uvas Canyon, too. "Leave in twenty?" he asks.

I nod, drain the last of my coffee, and race up the stairs to change.

Thirty minutes later, we step out of the house. I realize I'm on edge, my eyes flitting from left to right, scanning for suspicious characters — anyone out to vandalize our stuff or harass my family. It's silly, really, because they wouldn't be out and about in the open. But that's what all these incidents have done — they've instilled fear in me and this sense that we're not safe here anymore. I shake off the thoughts and join Jonas in the car.

Soon we reach the park and start trekking. The first few minutes pass in silence as we breathe in the fresh air and enjoy nature at its finest. It takes me back to those memorable mornings I spent hiking with my father. Those were the hours when he was the perfect father, the moments that gave me false hope that he had changed. That he would never make us suffer again. But it wouldn't take him long to prove me wrong — sometimes even before our next hike.

Since the quiet is polluting my mind with thoughts I can't tolerate, I start talking. Discussing Jonas's future, with him off to college. Speculating whether the Warriors will win another championship. Whether Purdy will do it for the 49ers. Will the Sharks ever get their act together?

"How are things with Val?" I ask once the sports talk tapers off. Valerie's his on-again, off-again girlfriend. They've known each other since middle school, and they first started dating sometime during high school.

He hesitates. "We're taking a break."

"Again?" Irritation flickers on his face for an instant. I kick myself for blurting that out without thinking.

"She ... she wants to take a break. I'm off to Georgia Tech. She's off to Washington State. It's going to be difficult maintaining a long-distance relationship."

"But it's doable. It's not like the old days where you had to wait weeks to get a letter, or pay through the nose to make a long-distance call. You can FaceTime or Zoom or whatever it is you kids do these days."

"I know. But it's college, Dad. We're going to meet new people, have new experiences. She wants us to have the freedom to explore."

"And you? Do you want the freedom, too?"

He shrugs. "Maybe. I don't know."

"She's an amazing girl. I like her. More importantly, she's good for you."

Valerie is respectful and affectionate, with a good head on her shoulders, unlike a lot of the teenagers I see around. She keeps Jonas grounded.

"I know, Dad. I know. I love her too."

Nothing more is said on the topic. Another lull in the conversation. The sun's out, and I stop to apply some sunscreen before resuming the hike. Eventually, Jonas breaks the silence.

"You working on a new book?"

"Yes."

"What's it about?"

"A woman investigating her sister's death. The cops insist it's suicide, but she's convinced it was murder. No one believes her."

"Interesting. But it's been done before, no?" In the last few years Jonas has taken a keen interest in my work. He has even helped me with some of my research, for which I'm grateful.

"It's a trope that's been used in the past, but not the way I'm approaching it."

"Ah, the Geraldi special sauce." His lips part into a grin.

I nod. It's heartening to see him happy. I wish he could always stay smiling this way.

"Isn't it too soon for another suicide story, though? *Shattered Lives* had one, too."

Pen's email swims in front of my eyes. I chickened out and never replied to her. Am I wrong in writing about such triggering topics? Somehow suicide is making it into everything I write recently, and I can't control it.

"Dad?"

I realize I've drifted off mentally. Jonas sounds concerned, and for his sake, I pull myself back to the present.

"I'm handling this one differently."

"Okay. You're the boss. Want me to research anything?"

"Not yet, but I'll come looking for you as soon as there's something."

"Cool."

Done with the sunscreen, I gulp some water before I start moving again. Jonas walks alongside me.

"Dad ..." His tone is grim this time. It's missing the casual lilt it usually carries.

The hesitation is evident on his face. I wonder what he wants to discuss. We've always been friends more than father and son. I've tried to maintain an open relationship where he feels comfortable talking to me about anything. That's how I know he has experimented with beer and vodka, and smoked weed. I know about every girl he has gotten close to, and how far he has gone with physical relationships. He has never hesitated to seek my advice. But this is making me nervous.

"What is it?" I ask, maintaining a calm voice.

"Dad ... is everything okay with you and Mom?"

It's like he has socked me in the gut. Does he know about me and Pen? Or is this about Heather and Patrick? Though things may seem messed up, Heather and I have had a fantastic relationship. Until now I've been sure the children have seen that. We rarely fight, and even when we do, it's not a nasty argument, and we try to avoid it when the kids are around. So I'm curious about what's compelling him to ask this question.

"Everything's great," I reply. "Why do you ask?"

"I ..."

The hesitation again. And then it hits me. I'm worrying too much. Perhaps this has nothing to do with us.

"Is this about Tyler?" I ask.

Tyler is Jonas's close friend, and his parents split up recently. That's probably what's on his mind. My question takes him by surprise. He's silent for a few moments.

"Yes. It ... it just got me worried, you know."

I can tell he's lying. I've blundered and missed my chance to discover what's really bugging him. He was already unsure, and by mentioning Tyler I've given him a way out. Now it may be impossible to ease the real reason out of him.

"Are you sure that's what's bothering you?"

"Yes, Dad."

I place a hand on his shoulder. "You can be frank with me. You know that, right?"

"I do, Dad."

"You have nothing to worry about. Heather and I are doing great." *Are we, though?*

And that's the end of that conversation. The rest of the hike passes mostly in silence, with short bursts of forced chatter. I'd hoped the time with my son would refresh me, but all it's done is fill me with fear — about what's bothering Jonas, and about what it means for me and my relationship with Heather.

On the way home, we pick up the minivan from the body shop. It looks as good as new with the fresh paint job. Jonas takes the Porsche, while I drive the van, hoping this is the last time there's an incident involving the cars.

There's a package sitting outside our front door when we arrive. My heart leaps, and I step up to the door trying to stay calm as my palms sweat. One glance at the box addresses some of my fears. This one has a mailing label. The relief is short-lived, though, because I don't recognize the sender, and I wonder whether Pen has stepped up her game by disguising her Trojan horse better this time.

I consider opening the package outside, in case there's a mess like last time, then decide against it. What will be will be. I pick up the package and carry it inside with trembling hands and place it on the kitchen counter, debating my next step. Eventually, my curiosity wins out. I take a deep breath and rip off the packing tape. Then I say a silent prayer and part the flaps.

No sound.

No explosion.

No splashes of crimson.

Just a bunch of security cameras. *Whew!* I take out the cameras and place them next to the box. There's an instruction sheet as well, which I skim over.

"Oh, great. Finally," says Heather when she sees everything spread out before me. "Should I call Raul to install these?"

I frown. As if I can't handle this by myself.

"Come on, you know you're not handy."

The fact is, she's right. I'm not. But I hate shelling out a fortune to a handyman for simple jobs like this one. We can afford it, but still. Nobody wants to part with their hard-earned money if they don't have to — not even the people with net worths upwards of eight figures. I'm no different. Now, if we needed a faucet replaced, or some woodwork done, sure. But not for this. I can handle it.

"Looks easy enough. I'll do it," I reply. "An hour tops."

She throws me a skeptical glance before walking away.

Four hours later I've got everything set up. Jonas had to help me with the technical stuff, but I handled all the hardware. I don't want to brag, but it looks like a professional installed the cameras. Even Raul couldn't do it this clean. Excited, I call Heather. She surveys my work and frowns.

"What?" I ask.

She points at my handiwork. "The paint."

I follow her finger to the small patches around the camera.

"It's hardly noticeable."

She sighs. "It looks awful, Daniel. Should have let Raul do it."

I want to fire off an angry response, but I resist. At least the job is done. We have functioning security cameras. These should be enough of a deterrent to anyone trying to harm or harass us at home. Even if they are stupid enough to do something, we'll have them on record and can ensure they are apprehended and punished appropriately. I take comfort in the fact that I've taken an important step towards keeping my family safe. I let go of my anger and exchange it for a relaxed breath.

21

DANIEL

Later that evening we're all seated for dinner, digging into the pasta marinara and garlic bread prepared by Heather. I love her cooking. The children do, too. I've just stuffed my mouth with some pasta when I have a fleeting thought — has she ever cooked for Patrick? Images of them flash before my eyes, with Heather feeding him as his ravenous eyes bore into her; Patrick setting the food aside and grabbing her, locking his lips on hers. It's a struggle, but I manage to block out the poison to focus on the present and these precious moments where we're relishing a meal together as a family. Other than the clatter of forks hitting plates, it's quiet. The perfect time for a Dad joke.

"Riddle me this, Joyce. Why was Cinderella so bad at soccer?"

The characteristic eye roll followed by the shrug. Ah, I love it!

"Come on, humor me."

"Because she lost her shoe?"

"Nah. Try again."

Another shrug. "I got nothing."

"Because she kept running away from the ball."

"Daaad," she goes.

Heather and Jonas are enjoying the scene. I take a moment, grateful for the delighted faces.

"Even I knew that one, dummy," says Jonas.

Joyce punches his shoulder, and he covers the spot with his hand, crying out in mock agony. "Ouch. You broke my arm, Cinderella."

Laughter all around. We return to quiet eating until Jonas breaks the silence.

"So, I was at this motel the other day."

"What motel?" I ask.

"You know the one on First Street? Sleepytime Motel."

My fork stops midair. I'm hoping this is just a coincidence and this conversation's not headed where I think it's headed. Way to mess up the happy meal. I glance at Heather. She has gone pale.

"What were you doing there?"

"Just meeting a buddy who works there." He forks some more pasta into his mouth before continuing. "Interesting place."

"How so?"

"Some dirty stuff going on. A lot of *lovers* spending time in those rooms."

He looks Heather straight in the eye as he says this. *He knows!* Why else would he bring this up? Why else would he look at her this way? Is this what he wanted to discuss on the hike?

"Why's that dirty? Probably just couples doing what people in love do."

I glance at Joyce. She's oblivious to what's going down here, and I envy her innocence. To be unsullied by all the filth in the world, especially the laying bare of her parents' frailties. May she never have to endure any of that.

From the corner of my eye I notice Heather stealing glances at me. She looks worried. She doesn't know that I already know, and she's probably terrified about what will happen once I find out.

"Well, these didn't look like legit couples, if you know what I mean. More like lowlifes sneaking around having affairs."

I shouldn't go down this path, but I can't resist. "And how do you know that?"

"I saw someone I know. She was there with someone she shouldn't have been with." Again, he glances at Heather as he says this.

Before I can say anything, she musters a response. "Who ... who was it?"

Jonas waits a few beats, a sneer playing on his lips, before waving her off. "Never mind."

He returns to his pasta. I'm not sure what was the point of this drama, but I'm relieved he didn't go further. Perhaps he needed to vent, let off some steam. He must have been devastated when he found out. We start off our lives looking up to our parents, thinking they can do no wrong. But the passage of time chips away at that facade. We see them for who they really are, with all their shortcomings — that they aren't the perfect beings we thought they were. But it's usually the little things — realizing that our parents aren't all-knowing, that they drive way past the speed limit and cheat on their diets without any qualms, that they're prone to a bit of lying and anger just like everyone else.

What Heather has done — it's not a trifle, and Jonas's reaction is not surprising. He still has me worried, though. His anger, if left untamed, could have serious consequences. I must talk to him before things get out of hand.

22

DANIEL

The next morning, Heather's pacing in our bedroom. I'm perched on the edge of the bed. The kids aren't home. She's nervous, and she's giving me the jitters. I speculate whether it's due to all the incidents, Jonas's mention of the motel, or if it's something else. Is she building up the courage to declare that she's leaving me for Patrick? That she wants a divorce? My stomach churns. I brace for the worst. How will I cope if I lose her?

She stops and meets my eyes, her hands clasped together. "I ... I have a confession to make."

I don't say a word, waiting for her to continue, though the suspense is killing me. *Stay still, my beating heart*, I order myself lest anxiety gets the better of me.

Her eyes tear up and unlock from mine, the guilt evident. "Daniel, I ... I had an affair."

Finally. She has finally confessed. I can't help parsing her statement further. She said "had." Does that mean it's all over between her and Patrick? A ray of hope breaks through the darkness inside me, but I try to suppress it to avoid disappointment. I wonder what compelled her to come clean. Was it the fact that Jonas is on to her? Is she worried he'll tell me, and she wants to ensure she beats him to it? Or did the guilt catch up with her?

Whatever the current situation with Patrick, it's a relief hearing her admit the truth. It's also infuriating. Though I've been aware of her infidelity, until this moment I could have convinced myself I was imagining things. But her confession makes it real.

Rage bubbles up inside me. I want to gloat. I want to raise my voice and tell her I already know, that she's not as smart as she thinks she is. But I resist. It might cause her to shut down before she gives me the details I crave. I must react in the way she expects — appear wounded by this revelation, which I have been since I learned of her infidelity. Those feelings just never found an outlet until now.

I'm on my feet in an instant.

"You what?" My voice has gone up a few decibels, and it reflects in the terror in Heather's eyes. I don't think she has ever seen me this mad. "You cheated on me?"

"I ... I'm so sorry, Daniel. It was a mistake. I see that now. I don't know what got into me."

"How could you, Heather? How could you?"

"It's all over now. It's all over." A pause. "I know this is a lot to ask, but can you forgive me?"

She looks so earnest, her pleading eyes making it difficult to deny her request. A part of me wants to say "Yes" and hug her tight. Tell her it's okay so that we can put this behind us and move on. But that won't do it. For my own sanity I must acknowledge what's eating me up inside. So I let go. All the anger that I've bottled up floods into the room. I'm furious at Heather. I'm furious at Patrick. And I'm furious at whoever's been messing with our lives. All of it comes out directed at my wife of twenty years.

"Forgive you? Are you out of your mind, you bitch?"

I regret the word as soon as it's out of my mouth. Heather shrinks back, her face a mixture of fear and shock. I loathe myself for stooping so low, for crossing a boundary that I had laid down. Worse, it transports me right back to my childhood, to all those occasions when my father spewed this among other foul words at my mother. She never had shock on her face — only terror, because she knew what was coming next, and that she had to brace for the blows that would rain on her. And I remember myself, so helpless as I cowered in a corner, berating myself for not being brave enough to protect her.

As I watch Heather, her countenance changes. For a moment, a smirk spreads across her face — the same expression she has when one of the children swears. And just as quickly she's raging.

"Don't you call me that! How dare you!" Heather's volume now matches mine. In an instant she has transformed from a fearful, remorseful woman to a fierce warrior. I've never seen her like this. "You don't have the right to. Not after what you've been up to, and not after I've put up with your flings all these years. You think I don't know what a lying piece of shit you really are?"

Her words deliver a hefty blow to my gut. A flurry of thoughts and emotions power through me. She knows. She has known all this time, and I had no idea. I thought I was careful. How did she find out? I feel awful. Miserable. Like I'm the lowest form of scum. What Heather did was wrong, but I'm just as guilty, if not more. Not only about what I've been doing with Pen. There were two others in the past — one-night stands. There were countless other temptations that I resisted over the years — that I'm proud to have been strong enough to resist — but it doesn't hide the fact that I did slip up on those two occasions, and that's unacceptable. It's also why I was unable to confront her about her indiscretion — the guilt rooted in my subconscious never allowed me to. Besides, learning that she's just as weak as me has been comforting in a way. It can be a burden sharing life with a morally superior being. Heather's higher moral plane highlighted my frailties and added to my disappointment in myself. But now we're equals. She has set me free, and in a strange way I realize I love her more than ever.

As furious as I was, this was no way to talk to her. I collapse to the floor, my body heaving with sobs. "I'm sorry. I'm so sorry." It's all I can say as I remain glued to the spot. A minute passes before I sense a presence beside me. She takes me in her warm embrace and I sink into her chest, still bawling my heart out.

"I feel terrible about what I did, Daniel. That's not me, you understand? I ... I got carried away. But why do you do what you do? Am I not enough?"

I look up at her, into those beautiful blue eyes. "You are enough. You've always been more than enough." Hearing those words out loud, it sounds like a cheesy line from a movie, but I mean it in all sincerity. I wipe my eyes with the sleeve of my t-shirt, having already soaked Heather's top. "I love you. You know that, right?"

She nods. Her eyes are moist.

"I know it's wrong, but sometimes I just can't control myself. I promise it will never happen again," I say.

"It better not. And I promise I'll never stray again."

"So you're really done with him?"

"Yes." The word soothes me. I let the ray of hope shine again. "That's why he's been doing all this. It's his way of getting back."

"Doing what?"

"The slashed tires. The graffiti. He didn't take it well when I told him it was over."

"Oh." This is an interesting development. "You sure he's the one behind it all?"

"Yes."

"The paint package too?"

Heather thinks for a moment. "No, that couldn't be him. We were still together when that happened."

Pen's still a strong candidate for the paint explosion. But that's a problem for another day. We gotta focus on lover boy first.

"Who is he?" I want to hear it from her.

Heather sighs hard. "Patrick. Joyce's soccer coach."

Her response confirms it. I was right all along. I suppress the urge to mock her judgment, to say *What were you thinking getting involved with a kid — your own daughter's coach.* Instead, I follow up with the burning question. "Why did you end it?"

"It just felt so wrong."

I know the feeling. It's how I was after both my encounters. The trysts were amazing, but I was miserable later. Racked with guilt and wishing I hadn't caved to my base urges. That's why I tried to push those memories out of my mind, those reminders of what a lowlife I was. Though the second one was harder to get rid of, because she got pregnant. I took care of the situation, of course, but it wasn't as easy, and it weighs on my conscience to this day.

"We should call the cops," I say. "We can't let him get away with it."

"They aren't going to be much help. You've seen what happened the two times we called them."

"Right, but that was before we knew who was doing this. We should at least get a restraining order so he doesn't dare mess with us again."

"I guess. But I'm more worried that Jonas knows about the affair. How do we handle that?"

I try my best to fake surprise. We may have kissed and made up, but I'm not putting all my cards on the table just yet. "He knows?"

"Yes. Remember the stuff he was telling us about that motel last night?"

"Sleepytime Motel? The lovers?"

She nods.

"Is that where you ..."

"Yes. That's where we used to meet."

"And you didn't see Jonas there any time?"

"No. Never."

"We'll tell him it's all a misunderstanding. We'll figure out what to say."

"You think he'll believe us? He's a smart cookie, you know."

"Yes, but he will if we're convincing enough. Don't worry. I'll talk to him."

I've assured Heather I can handle Jonas, but that's a tough hill to climb. First, I want the restraining order so that we're safer. It's something I've researched before for one of my novels. Now that we're proceeding with it, I have to refresh my memory about the details. I grab the laptop sitting on the bed and review the instructions on the website again.

An hour later we're dressed and on our way to the Santa Clara County Superior Court in downtown San Jose. It's comforting to be taking some action, to get back at Patrick. I hope this step keeps my family secure and serves as a severe warning to him.

At the court, Heather takes a seat while I fill out the forms. It's tedious work, and it's a relief once I've submitted the paperwork. The clerk is confident we'll have a response tomorrow. At best, the judge will grant a temporary restraining order and set a date for the hearing. We'll still have to gather evidence to present at the hearing. While we do have pictures of the damage inflicted, there's nothing in there that proves that Patrick was responsible.

"We need proof that he did all that," I say to Heather as we drive back. "Otherwise the protection expires after twenty-one days."

She's quiet for a while, and I feel despondent. Then she speaks. "He sent me messages. Would those work?"

"What kind of messages?"

"Threats. I'll show you once we're home."

"Here," Heather says as soon as I've settled on the couch. She's holding out her phone.

I take it from her. She sits next to me. I'm curious, but I'm also dreading what I'll see.

> P: I miss u.

> P: I luv u.

> P: y don't u answr

I cringe, not just at the content, but the appalling spellings, too. *Is it so hard to spell out everything correctly?* He sounds like a whiny teenager. How could Heather fall for a dumbbell like that? Are his good looks so overwhelming? Or am I so disgusting that even trash like him is a better option? The guy has no chance in hell of getting his paws on my wife anymore, but hatred for him swells inside me. I force myself to stay calm and focused. These first texts are a few hours apart, presumably soon after she dumped him. Still harmless. But it doesn't take long for things to turn ugly.

> P: u btch!

> P: im gonna hrt u so bad

> H: Stop it! We are done!!!

There are tons of such messages. All talk, no action, though. I can't imagine how Heather handled all of this without losing her mind, keeping it bottled up inside. Perhaps if she had reached out to me earlier we could have avoided the problems that followed.

But I don't blame her. She probably thought it would die down. That Patrick would get over it and move on.

"It's from the day he slashed the tires," she says.

While it's not conclusive proof that Patrick had anything to do with it, it sure seems he did it.

She's not a tree, you idiot! I want to scream, though I know he means "popular." I don't have to be a genius to figure out that this message is from the day he spray-painted our van and part of the neighborhood with Heather's number. I'm aching to grab the schmuck and punch him with all my might. To see him bleed, that pretty face bruised and beaten. Maybe knee him in the groin so hard that he dare not mess with another married woman again.

I push those thoughts out of my mind and focus on the task at hand — compiling all this evidence in an organized manner so that it's effective enough to convince the judge. It's only when I'm done that I rest easy.

23

—·—

DANIEL

*I*t was a dark and stormy night.

    I stare at the sentence on my laptop screen and sigh. After an hour of furious typing and flowing words, I've reached a standstill with my writing session. This clichéd line is proof that I'm stuck. I'm almost tempted to leave it in, curious to see how my editor reacts when she reads it. But I'll spare her the pain. I can do better.

Fiona scrambled down the trail cautiously as gusts of wind threatened to push her off the path. The moisture in the air told her that rain wasn't far away, and she didn't have much time. If only the moon wasn't hiding behind the clouds, she would be able to move faster.

I review my latest effort. Not bad for a first draft. This will have to do for now. This is the scene I'd envisioned when I was at Rancho that fateful night. If I can get the words to match my vision, that blow to the head will have been worth it.

I take a bite of soft, warm banana bread and wash it down with a sip of cappuccino. Baristas who offer to heat the bread before serving it are angels in disguise. These angels are one of the reasons

I love visiting Barefoot Café. While I do most of my writing in my office, it helps to escape my cave occasionally and work outside. The change of scenery jogs my creative cells, and watching a variety of people milling about produces a flurry of ideas.

There's so much material within the confines of this establishment. Like the woman at the corner table. She seems to be in her sixties. She has an oversized mug of coffee on the table and dunks her cookies in the beverage before taking a bite. There's a look of childlike bliss and contentment as she does so, and it's adorable. I could leave it at that, but the darkness within me, or perhaps the thriller author inside me, gives the scene a menacing spin. She's happy because she slipped poison into the tea of her husband of forty years before leaving home. It's something the cops won't be able to detect, and they'll pin his death on heart failure due to old age. When she returns from the café she'll call 911 and fake grief and heartbreak for a few weeks, while cackling inside.

Then there's the young couple at the table opposite. The way they've been gazing at each other, they seem to be on a date — early days in the relationship. It's early in the day for a date, if you ask me, but perhaps they spent a passionate night together and are out for breakfast. And then I do it again. They aren't single. They're having an affair and are cheating on their spouses. This is a clandestine rendezvous. Sadly, it reminds me of Heather and Patrick and my mood sours.

"Mowgli," the barista calls out, and just like that my mood brightens. I can't help but chuckle as I realize whose order is up. A few minutes ago an Indian guy was placing his order, repeatedly clarifying his name was Murali. Clearly, his point didn't get through.

All the people-watching and amusing occurrences are great, but there's one problem with working in a place like this. The distractions. There's this stunning woman bussing the tables. She's my type — long dark hair, and a slender, curvy body. Young, with flawless skin. She even has a tattoo on her forearm, an anchor, and the promise of more tattoos in places I cannot see — yet. I'm so tempted to strike up a conversation with her, but I'm trying to be my best self, especially after the heart-to-heart with Heather. It's a real struggle sometimes. I take another bite of the delicious bread and try to focus on the screen.

It's at times like this that I understand my father and his temptations. He knew, and I do too, that these temptations are inappropriate and must be avoided, but we still succumb to them, no matter how hard we try. For him it was the lure of the bottle; for me it's the siren call of an attractive woman. I just hope I don't end up at the bottom of the stairs, dead, like him. It shouldn't come to that, because, unlike him, I would never hurt anyone. Not physically, anyway. I've emotionally wounded Heather, but it's not the same as the damage my father inflicted on his family.

Sometimes I worry if this weakness, this inability to resist the temptations, is hereditary. My father passed something on to me, and I'll pass it on to Jonas. Jonas is a good kid and seems to have dodged this bullet, but who knows?

Now that my attention has been drawn to weaknesses, I recollect my first stumble. The day I was lapping up the dregs of my coffee at this same café when a woman approached me. She could barely contain her excitement as she introduced herself as Selena, asking me if I was the famous author Daniel Geraldi. At the time I was unaccustomed to such attention outside of signing events. To be recognized by a fan out in the wild was a huge boost to my ego.

She invited me to her apartment a block away, telling me she had my entire collection, asking me whether I would mind signing it all. I should have declined, but Heather and I had argued that morning — she had insinuated that I wasn't helping around the house as much, a claim that I disagreed with. I was still harboring resentment towards her, and the opportunity to spend time with a ravishing fan who had only good things to say about me was too tempting to pass up.

It was an innocent visit at first. Selena brought out the hardcovers, all in mint condition, and I signed them all. I was headed out the door when it started raining. She brought out a bottle of wine while I waited for the downpour to stop. By the time we drained the bottle, her hand had found mine, stirring something inside me. I followed her as she led me to the bed. It was like I was in a trance, and it wasn't until the deed was done and we lay back, satisfied, that the extent of my blunder hit me. I sobbed like a baby, racked with guilt about what I had done to Heather. As I walked out of the apartment, I resolved never to stray again. I was true to that promise until a few years later — my second stumble, but I can't bear going there.

My phone buzzes just as Fiona's about to reach her destination. It's Heather. I almost ignore the call, not wanting to interrupt my flow, but a voice inside me implores me to answer. So I do. Fiona will have to stay put a bit longer. She's tough — she'll survive.

"Daniel … get here quick. Something … something's happened." Panic laces Heather's voice. Fear too. It's contagious, but I try to remain calm, thankful that I decided to take the call.

"What happened, hon?"

"Just … just get here. Please!"

I grab the laptop with my sweaty palms, dump the food, and sprint to the car. My heart's galloping. Knowing Heather's in a terrible state is bad enough, but it's worse not knowing what I'll face when I make it home.

I speed all the way, eyes darting to the rearview mirror every few seconds for any signs of a cop car. The last thing I need now is to be pulled over and handed a speeding ticket. But I make it to my street without incident. When I approach my home my heart lurches and the coffee and bread scamper up my throat, threatening to spring forth at any moment, because there's a beat-up Accord parked outside. The situation must be bleak if Patrick's inside. *Has he harmed Heather? Am I too late?*

I turn into the driveway and dash out of the car. The front door's ajar. Another bad sign. The first thing I see when I enter the living room — a sight I wish I could unsee — that I wish were a dream and not reality — the rug soaked in blood, the coffee table on top of it, the glass smashed, and on the base of the table — a lifeless body. I stop dead in my tracks, unable to turn away, unsure about what to do next. Something tells me that, like the glass, our lives are shattered forever, never to be whole again. It takes quite an effort to scan the rest of the room. Heather's on the couch, sobbing, with her head in her hands. I advance towards the body for a closer inspection. It's Patrick.

Whenever I imagined him getting beaten up or in pain, it filled me with immense joy. But there's none of that now. I'm just horrified. We were so traumatized when that package exploded and spread crimson paint everywhere. That was tame in contrast to all the real blood around me now.

"Heather." I barely croak her name out.

She looks up at me with a devastated expression that I know will haunt me forever. I rush to her side, avoiding the mess in the middle. She hugs me tight, like I'll slip away if her grip slackens. She whimpers into my shoulder for what seems like an eternity. I comfort her, but every second is painful, because I'm desperate to know what happened. Finally she parts from me and gazes into my eyes.

"It ... it was an accident. I ... I didn't mean to ..."

I nod, as if she needs me to confirm that she's not a heartless killer. Maintaining a calm voice, I say, "Tell me what happened."

"I ... I was busy in the kitchen when I heard a knock. By the time I washed my hands to get to the door, it was too late."

"What do you mean it was too late?"

"He was already inside. In the kitchen."

"How did he get inside? Wasn't the door locked?"

Heather goes pale. It's not the first time she's forgotten to lock the door in spite of my repeated reminders. In the past I've lost my cool on finding out, and she probably fears another outburst from me. The fact is, I'm furious, especially considering that this time the lapse has had fatal consequences. But I take a deep breath. This is not the time for an argument.

"Okay. So the door was unlocked. He got inside. Then what?"

"He pleaded with me to take him back. I refused. Then he got agitated, and I slipped out to the living room. He followed. He grabbed my shoulders and ..." Heather's crying again. "He tried to kiss me. I pushed him away. He tripped over the rug ... and ... and ..."

She's unable to finish, but I get the picture. The fall itself couldn't have killed him, but a couple of sharp edges of glass did a number on his neck and he bled out. I detest glass tables, but Heather loves them. I prefer solid wood all the way, not only for the elegant appearance, but because it's safer, something that was important when the children were younger. Now this glass table has caused irreparable harm. I could never have imagined that life would be better with Heather having an affair rather than with her breaking it off. This jackass didn't take rejection well.

"Have you called the cops?" I ask.

She shoots me a horrified look. "What? No! Are you crazy?"

"We'll explain. We'll tell them it was an accident. Thanks to the restraining order they already know he was harassing you. They'll understand."

"No, Daniel! No f— *damn* way. They'll haul me away. I can't deal with that. We have to manage this ourselves."

It takes me a moment to grasp what she's suggesting.

"You mean we hide the body? Are you kidding me? You think we can get away with that? We'll be in a bigger hole if we do that."

"I've given it a lot of thought. We don't have a choice, Daniel." She's pleading with her eyes. "Now, are you going to help me or not?"

I'm quiet for what seems like an eternity. "I still feel—"

"No, Daniel. Just think it through like I have. If we call the cops, there's no way this goes well. It doesn't matter what we explain, if they're doing their job right they will investigate. They will suspect us, might even arrest us."

She pauses, catching my bemused expression. "Yes, even you, Daniel. He was the guy your wife was having an affair with — you have the strongest motive to get rid of him. And—"

"In my experience, when a man kills his wife's lover, he kills his wife, too. No one will believe I murdered him."

"Okay, fine. Maybe they'll only suspect me, but you're missing the point. It doesn't matter if they eventually conclude it's an accident and they let me go, the damage will have been done. Everyone we know will still consider me with suspicion. And what's worse, if there's an investigation, word of the affair will get out. Imagine the headlines — *Beloved Soccer Coach Found Dead in Lover's Home*. Think about what that will do to our reputation, how it will devastate our children. We won't be able to live here anymore."

She has made some compelling arguments, but her suggestion still sounds like one of the trainwreck decisions that a character from one of my novels would make. I mull over our options, weighing the risk, though I know she's going to win out like she always does. "Yes, of course I'll help. But I still think it's a terrible idea."

The situation is somewhat familiar. It takes me back to that day — what, thirty or so years ago? My father sprawled at the bottom of the stairs, dead, with me staring up at my mom who was standing at the top of the staircase. The look of horror on her face which, even at that tender age, I deduced was not because of what she had done, but because I had caught her doing it. A part of me was repulsed. That man may have made our lives miserable, but he was a decent human most of the time — he took me on transcendent hikes and spoiled me silly with scoops of ice cream. He didn't deserve to die, did he? No, my little mind debated — he did merit some punishment since he didn't really care about us. If he cared enough, he wouldn't verbally abuse us, wouldn't physically harm us. People would suggest that we could have walked away, but it wasn't so simple. He would never have left us in peace. So while a part of me found it hard to stomach what my mom had done, another part of me was proud of her. Proud that the meek woman I'd known my entire life had grown bold enough to fight back.

I hadn't felt any pressure that day — me, just a child. It was my mom's responsibility, and she would do whatever was necessary. She called 911 and told them it was an accident. The investigation concluded quickly and life went on. A much better life, I must admit, barring the nightmares that have haunted me since.

But I can't stand by and watch someone else handle the situation today. I must be at the forefront of the response. I still believe we should call 911 and spill the truth, but now that Heather has shot down that idea, it complicates things. While I contemplate my next move, questions swirl in my mind. Patrick was sleeping with my wife — a married woman. He was harassing us. He deserved to die, right? Maybe not? After all, he was an acceptable soccer coach, beloved by his students. At least, that's how Joyce puts it. Joyce, Joyce — I worry about her. How will she react when she finds out Patrick's gone forever?

Sweeping those thoughts away, I spring into action, pulling on gloves and handing a pair to Heather. We must clear this mess before the children return. I roll the corpse onto the rug and move the table out of the way. We roll the body in the rug and clean everything with bleach, scrubbing away traces of blood and tossing the glass and tissues in a trash bag. Then we move it all to the garage and wait for nightfall.

"So, about the body," I say once I'm settled on the couch. Heather's spraying air freshener to mask the scent of bleach. "We could dissolve it in acid."

Her eyes widen in alarm.

"Brutal. I know. There's another option, but I can't stand the thought of chopping him to bits. We could just bury him in the woods."

The saner option restores her face to normal. She ponders over my suggestion before replying. "No. We should just dump the body somewhere far away, but easy enough to find."

"Why? That doesn't make any sense."

"If he has a family — they'll need closure. They just can't go on not knowing where he is. We can't torture his family like that. They didn't harm us in any way."

I shake my head. "You're out of your mind, Heather. You don't even know if he has a family."

"He probably does. His parents might still be alive. He also mentioned a Sylvia once." Heather shudders. "God, I hope he wasn't married." A pause. "What if he had kids?"

"Should have called the cops if you care so much about this imaginary family of his. Finding the body won't give them closure. They'll still be in the dark about how he died."

She shrugs. "Too late for that now that we've messed with the crime scene. We just have to do the best we can."

I open my mouth to reply but one glance at her forces it shut. Her arms are crossed, and her face is set in an all-too-familiar expression — an interesting combination of a pout and quivering lips, with her eyes brimming with tears. It's a pointless battle. Against my better judgment, I cave. We'll do as she says and take our chances.

The children arrive a few minutes later and stare at the suddenly roomy living room.

"What happened here?" Joyce asks.

"Looks kinda cool," Jonas adds. "I love the open space."

I thought I was mentally prepared to deal with the questions, but I'm nervous. I notice that Heather is, too. Joyce does raise a good point, and if the missing pieces make her question what's up, anyone else who has been here before will perceive it too. We must get a new table and rug pronto.

"Your mom thinks we need a change. Time to redecorate. We'll get new stuff." I'd like to believe I said that in an even tone with not a hint of nerves.

"But didn't we just buy new stuff last year?" Like me, Jonas is practical.

"I agree with Mom. I was getting bored of that rug. We needed the change." Joyce sounds just like Heather.

Discussion complete, they depart to their rooms. Heather heaves a sigh of relief. I collapse on the couch and lean back. A part of me is delighted that Patrick got what he had coming. I only wish I could have been the one to deliver the fatal blow.

"Oh!" I say, as I remember something.

"What?" she asks, looking concerned.

"His car. It's still outside. We should move it before anyone sees it."

"It's kinda late for that, isn't it? Pretty sure half the street has already seen it. Besides, it will be worse if someone sees us moving it. Not that anyone's going to notice a beat-up Accord. It doesn't exactly stick out like a yellow Lamborghini."

She's right. We must wait until dark. "But we'll need the key."

Heather frowns. "Oh."

"Yeah. We'll have to search his pockets."

She nods. Then her eyes widen.

"What?" It's my turn to play the guessing game.

"His phone. We need his phone too. The cops can track it. They'll know he was here."

"Can't do much about that now. We just have to ensure the phone moves with his body."

"Right."

That's the end of our conversation.

Later, we get through dinner somehow. Heather wasn't in a state to cook, so we ordered pizza. The children loved it, while Heather and I struggled to push the slices down our nervous throats. We would have skipped the meal completely, but it was important to maintain the illusion of normalcy to avoid alarming the children.

Once they're off to bed, we get to work. Donning a fresh pair of gloves, I unroll the rug and stare at the lifeless form before me. It gives me the creeps, but what must be done must be done. I search Patrick, gingerly at first, as if he's asleep and I dare not wake him up. Eventually, I fish out the car key from his jeans pocket. The successful rush doesn't last long, because I can't find his phone. I fear we might have dropped it somewhere in the house. But the first priority is to move his body and car out of here. So I wrap him in the rug again and step out of the garage to join Heather.

It's pleasant outside. On any other night I would have stood here and breathed in the cool, fresh air, probably invited her for a stroll around the neighborhood. That's the last thing on my mind tonight.

It's past midnight, and as expected, she confirms there's no activity. But I still scout the area myself to be on the safe side. For a moment I think there's movement a few houses down the street, but when there's nothing else I figure it's just nerves and I imagined it. Once I'm convinced that the coast is clear, we haul the body out to stuff it in the minivan. I would have preferred to transport it in Patrick's car, but there's no way it would fit in there while wrapped in the rug. It's hard work. The corpse is heavy, and we're panting by the time we unload it. I return to the garage to grab the trash bag.

My heart takes a leap when I see the bag. Someone has tampered with it. I scan the garage and I'm shocked to see Jonas standing in a corner, arms crossed over his chest.

"What ... what are you doing here?" It's all I can muster.

"What's going on, Dad? It's like someone died in here."

"I ..."

"It's okay. I saw you and Mom haul the body. And I've seen what's in the bag. That, and the whole thing with the rug and the table, I know something's up."

I'm surprised he isn't freaking out.

"It was an accident," I reply.

"Then why all the hush-hush?"

"It may not look good for us."

"Interesting. Just like something out of one of your novels." He uncrosses his arms and takes a few steps towards me. His eyes are bright and eager. "Who is it, anyway?"

"The less you know the better. In case someone investigates."

"Don't worry about me. I can handle myself. Tell me, who is it?"

I hesitate a bit before caving, knowing he's smart enough to figure it out eventually. There's no point delaying the inevitable.

"It's Patrick."

Jonas arches an eyebrow. "Patrick. *Patrick*, Patrick? Joyce's soccer coach?"

I nod and wipe a river of sweat from my forehead.

"You killed him, didn't you, Dad?"

"No! Why would I?"

"Come on, Dad. I know he was screwing ... sorry ... I know he was involved with Mom. I would have wrung the bastard's neck myself if I had the chance."

There it is. No hesitation, no vague hints. Just out with the brutal truth. It stings, but I appreciate it. This is the kind of relationship I've always had with Jonas, the level of openness I want to maintain with him. Of course, I flinch at the crude language, but, tonight, I'm in no position to reprimand him. My head swims. I already know the answer, but I present the question anyway.

"How ... how do you know they were involved?"

"I saw them at the motel."

This confirms it. Heather's choice of love nest was atrocious. Jonas and I both caught her there. I wonder who else must have seen her. Are there others who know what misdeeds she'd been up to?

"She made a mistake. But it was over a while back."

"Well, that's a relief." His tone is dripping with sarcasm. "Still a huge mistake. Is that why you killed him?"

"I told you — it was an accident."

"Well, good riddance." He's grinning. A man died a gruesome death in our house. I would have expected shock, dismay. But he's enjoying this. I shudder. Maybe I don't know my son as well as I thought. Then I remember the time last year when a rat had been menacing our garage for weeks. Jonas found it one morning and whacked it on the head. The blood and gore forced me to look away, but he cleaned up the mess looking quite pleased with himself. Perhaps I shouldn't be surprised at his behavior. Still, there's a big difference between a human and a rodent, though considering what Patrick had been doing with Heather, he wasn't much better than a rodent.

Jonas turns pensive. "But poor Joyce will take it hard."

"Yes, she will." The reminder is like a stab to my heart.

"You need any help with the clean up here?"

"Thanks, but we're good. Go upstairs. Get some sleep. It's better you don't get involved." I pick up the trash bag. "Oh, and please don't tell your mother you know. She'll worry."

"You still care about her."

"Of course. She's my wife."

"A wife who's been cheating on you."

I want to explain to him that marriage can be complicated. Relationships can be difficult. We're all humans, and we make mistakes. But this is not the time. I have more urgent problems to resolve.

"We'll talk later."

He turns to go but stops. "The couch," he says.

"What about it?"

"It's got some blood spatter."

Damn!

"Want me to take care of it? I know a guy."

"Okay," I say reluctantly as I return to the minivan to stash the bag, wondering why he has a blood removal expert on speed dial.

"What took you so long," Heather hisses when I finally join her outside.

"Sorry. I just needed a moment."

"We don't have time for any *moments*."

I'm tempted to snipe at her, but I don't engage. We must see this through as a team. Conflict will only cause everything to fall apart.

We've got the body, the rug, and the trash. The table stays in the garage, since it won't fit in the minivan. We'll figure out how to dump it. Anyway, we scrubbed it well so it shouldn't draw any suspicion.

I'm about to get inside Patrick's car when a thought strikes. I walk over to Heather. She's already belted in, ready to drive off.

"I think you should drive his car. I'll take the van."

"Why?" She sounds exasperated, as if she's still mad about my delay. This imposition doesn't help.

"Whoever drives his car will shed some DNA. If this ever comes back to us, they will try to match our DNA with whatever they find in there," I reply, pointing to the Accord. "I won't be able to justify why I was in there, but you could always say you've been in his car."

Heather considers my suggestion for a bit before nodding. "Good thinking." Her approval gladdens my heart. I'm like a puppy who thrives on keeping her happy.

She gets out of the van and we walk over to the Accord. Once inside, she rifles inside the center console and holds up something.

I'm relieved to see Patrick's cell phone. She tries to turn it on, but it seems the battery is drained. I wonder whether that happened before he reached our place or while he was inside. The former option is appealing. In either case, leaving the phone where it is is the best option. Heather fires up the Accord and drives away. I follow in the minivan.

Our first stop is at Rancho San Antonio Park. Memories of my last visit give me the shivers. As if our current mission isn't scary enough. I would have picked a different dumping ground, but Heather suggested it and I couldn't come up with a convincing reason for avoiding it.

Rancho is desolate, as expected. We take a minute to scan the surroundings and listen for any indication that anyone is around. Once we're convinced that we're alone, we lift the corpse out of the Odyssey and unroll the rug. We stuff the body in the trunk of Patrick's car. It's difficult bending his stiff form to make it fit, but we make it work. We'll leave his Accord here for someone to find. Then we roll the rug and put it back in the minivan. The rug was important to hide the corpse during transportation, but we can't risk having our stuff found near it. Heather joins me in the minivan. Then we drive off, riding in silence all the way.

Next stop is at Hellyer park. We toss the rug in the creek and the trash bag in the lake. Then we return home. My heart's been racing all this time, and it takes a while before it settles into its regular rhythm. I feel filthy. A hot shower helps somewhat, but I find it difficult to sleep. So does Heather. We just lie in bed, her head on my chest, with me stroking her back. At some point I drift off into the welcome embrace of unconsciousness.

24

DANIEL

I awake to a terrifying realization — we've been sloppy. We transported Patrick's bloody body in the minivan, and it must have left traces of his DNA in there. I've got to clean it up before it's too late.

Five minutes later I'm crouched inside the Odyssey, bleaching every nook and cranny. Once I'm satisfied with my handiwork, I drive the van to a full-service car wash for another thorough clean as additional protection. Besides, I hope it suppresses the odor of bleach. It's only when I get home that I sit down for a hearty breakfast.

Later that day I drive Joyce to soccer practice. I know what's in store for us, but it's important we make it appear like nothing's happened. In the meantime, Heather's browsing the local furniture stores for a new couch, coffee table, and rug. Jonas's guy helped clean up the couch, but we're getting rid of it anyway. We don't want any reminders of the tragedy.

The mood is subdued when we reach the field, because Patrick isn't there. After a few minutes of waiting, the parents and children gripe about it and leave. So do we.

The next morning Joyce learns through the grapevine that Patrick still hasn't shown up to work and isn't responding to calls and texts. It's suspected that he's missing. She seems dejected. A wave of guilt passes through me. Joyce loves soccer, and she adores Patrick as a coach. She'll be devastated once she finds out the truth about what happened to him. I tamp down the guilty feeling — it's not like I killed the guy. It was an accident, I remind myself.

One more day is all it takes before the storm hits. There's a knock on the door, and I open it to find a man standing outside. He flashes his badge. A homicide detective. Detective Sanchez. This can't be good, and it makes me nauseous. He's so skinny, I imagine myself blowing and his body taking flight, soaring far, far away from me, never to return. If only it was so easy to make problems disappear.

"Mr. Geraldi?" he asks.

"Yes, that's me."

"Mind if I come inside? I have a few questions for you."

"About what?" I can't resist the question, though there's no doubt what he's here for. By this time Heather has joined me. I sense the fear pulsing through her. As I wipe my palms on my pants, I wonder whether she's sweating too. What's our fate if Sanchez discovers the truth? *Perhaps he already has, and that's why he's here?* What will happen to our children? That's the thought that worries me the most.

He glances at her before returning his gaze to me. "Do you know Patrick Delgado?"

"Patrick ..." I'm distracted by the thought that I know someone with the same last name. But who, I can't remember.

"Yes. He's our daughter's soccer coach." Heather takes over. Her tone is surprisingly even, given the circumstances. Impressive.

"He was reported missing yesterday."

"Oh. That's why he didn't show up for practice," I say, trying to stay calm and maintain the illusion of innocence. But I can't resist taking a dig at him.

"So this is what it takes to get SJPD to turn up."

"What do you mean?" Sanchez asks.

"Someone has to die or go missing before you bother to investigate. Any other problems and you don't give a damn."

"I'm sorry, I still don't get it."

"We've reported multiple incidents over the last few months. Someone slashed all our tires. Defaced our car. Left a dangerous package at our door. No one bothered to come."

Well, technically, we didn't report the package incident, but my argument still stands.

"I understand how that can be frustrating, Mr. Geraldi, but I'm sure you are aware of the situation. We simply don't have the resources to investigate everything. We're stretched thin when it comes to manpower. We prioritize cases related to safety and security."

"And what I just told you doesn't fall under that category?"

"Was anyone harmed?"

"No, not physically."

"Well, then."

"But it could have happened. This person came to our house multiple times. He hasn't attacked us yet, but he easily could have. It may just be the next step. Why do you guys have to be so reactive all the time?"

Sanchez shrugs. "It is what it is, Mr. Geraldi. Unfortunately, I can't help you there. Now, may I come in?"

Having burnt off some nervous energy with my rant, I move aside and he enters. He follows Heather to the living room, with me in tow. The couch is still there, but without the rug and table the area looks empty. She ordered the new furniture, but it won't arrive until next week. Sanchez stares at the space. *What's going on in his head? Does he know this is where Patrick breathed his last?* I picture crime scene tape surrounding the area. Heather and me being led off in handcuffs. The children watching, eyes brimming with tears. I shake the nightmare out of my head.

"We're redecorating." She fills the silence.

He nods and settles on one end of the couch. I take the other end. Heather remains standing, hands clasped together, looking unsure about what to do. I tilt my head slightly. She takes my hint and drops into the loveseat.

"When did you see him last?" he asks.

"Last week at soccer practice," I reply. Heather's been avoiding it for a while now, so I've been taking Joyce. I was hoping Patrick would get fired or at least suspended due to the restraining order, but that never happened.

"And you?" Sanchez turns to Heather.

"Hmm ... let me see ..." She takes her time replying. So smooth. But I shouldn't be surprised. If there's one thing I've learned in the past few weeks, it's that my wife's a darn good liar. "It's been a while. A few weeks, I think."

"So this would be before you filed the restraining order?"

So he knows about that. Of course he does. He's a cop. A cop who has done his homework. We're skating on thin ice. A tornado brews in my belly.

"Yes. That's right," Heather replies.

"I read through your request. It seems like Delgado made some threats, but there were no direct attacks. There were a couple of concerning incidents, but how did you know he was behind them?"

"I know it was him. I just know. He did threaten me when ... when I ended it with him. And he also called and texted me a few times after that with threats."

"Do you have any proof? I didn't see any in your request."

"Yes. We have texts from him that we're planning to present as evidence."

"I see. So as I understand it, you have plenty of motive to see him disappear."

Sanchez finally gets to the point. The real reason he is here. We're his prime suspects, not just people he's interviewing to gather information.

"I ..." Heather has gone pale. This is not the time to lose her nerve, but I can't blame her. She has been handling it quite well until now. "I could never hurt anyone."

"I didn't say he's hurt. Just missing."

"I know, but ..."

"Detective, I can assure you we don't have anything to do with his disappearance." I step in to help her out.

Sanchez turns to me. "Mr. Geraldi, did you know your wife was involved with Delgado?"

"Yes, I did."

"And how did that make you feel?"

"Awful. As you would expect any husband to feel."

"You must hate Delgado. You probably have a much stronger motive than even your wife."

He's right. I've pictured myself squeezing Patrick's throat several times until he was blue, but I wouldn't have killed him, unless it was in self-defense. Especially not after Heather ended things. What would be the point?

"I did hate him, yes. And I was furious after he did those things. But as I said earlier, I didn't harm him in any way."

Sanchez considers our responses for a bit before speaking. "As of this morning, Patrick Delgado is no longer considered a missing person." He pauses, clearly for effect, because he gives us each a glance, watching our reaction, before continuing. "He's dead."

"Oh." I muster what I think is the appropriate response of shock and surprise for this revelation. Heather does one better with a gasp, her hand going up to her mouth. Inside, I'm trembling.

Sanchez is playing games, since he initially told us Patrick was missing, and only now did he reveal that Patrick's dead. I should have caught on to that earlier. Why else would they send someone from Homicide instead of Missing Persons? This subterfuge confirms something — he suspects us, and he's trying to get us to trip up.

"His body was found at Rancho San Antonio Park."

"How did he die?" I ask.

"We're still looking into that."

It won't take them long to figure out the cause of death, and Patrick's cell phone location data will tell them that our home was the last place he visited. *Did we make a mistake by not dumping the body somewhere it wouldn't be found?* It's tempting to blame this on Heather, but the fact is, they would have looked up his location data even if he was only a missing person. We're in trouble either way. I wonder whether Sanchez already has the data and he's just messing with us, waiting for either one of us to stumble.

"Do you know anyone who would want to harm him?" he continues.

I give it some thought, as does Heather. "No," we shake our heads and reply in unison.

"If there's nothing else, I'll get going," he says as he stands up. "Here's my card. Call me if you remember anything that could help our investigation."

Relief floods Heather's face as she takes the card from him. The same sensation is coursing through me, though I know this is only a temporary reprieve. Sanchez will be back for sure, and when he does, we better be prepared.

25

DANIEL

Joyce was ... a mistake. I risk sounding like a heartless monster, but it's true. Heather and I were overwhelmed after Jonas was born, and those first years of his life stressed me out. That time was an endless stream of sleepless nights, frustrating feeding sessions, and revolting diapers. Exhausted all the time, we snapped at each other so much that I worried our marriage wouldn't make it. While it was obvious raising a child was no joke, I didn't realize how difficult a job it was until I was trapped in the middle of it. Not to mention expensive. So I was clear I didn't want more children, and I thought Heather was on the same page.

It was a shock when she told me she was pregnant again. Even more of a jolt when she insisted she wanted the baby. I was too weak to share my opinion, and we went ahead with it. A few more rough years followed once she was born, a rehash of the miserable Jonas years — worse, actually, since now we had two little ones to take care of. But when I look at her today, I'm so grateful that we have her. She's an amazing girl — so thoughtful, so loving and caring.

I can't wait for her to blossom into an amazing woman. My life would have been incomplete without her.

So it hurts to see her like this, grieving the loss of her beloved soccer coach. We broke the news to her after Sanchez left, figuring it was better she heard it from us rather than from some other source. She was devastated, as expected. All this for someone who wasn't even all that great at his job. At least, that's what I gleaned from the little bit I've seen him at work. Of course, it's probably not his coaching skills as much as his personality and pleasant nature that is being mourned here. I don't have any personal experience of this, but that's what I conjecture based on what I hear from my little girl. If she only knew this is the same man who was boning her mother behind my back, perhaps she wouldn't be so sad. She might even be furious.

But I let her grieve in innocence. She shouldn't have to bear the burden of our marital issues. She'll get over it eventually. That is, assuming Heather and I don't land in trouble for our sins.

26

DANIEL

Two days. That's all it takes for Sanchez to return to our abode. This time he has a smug air about him, and it shakes me to the core. If I could just huff and puff and blow him away. But this ain't *Three Little Pigs*.

I lead him inside. Heather's in the kitchen, cooking, and she freezes when she spots him. They exchange greetings before he turns his attention to the living room. Our new couch, coffee table, and rug are in place.

"Looks nice," he remarks, his face matching his vapid tone.

"Thank you," I reply. "Heather has great taste."

His eyes scan the room, as if searching for clues. It makes me uneasy.

"Why don't you sit down." I gesture to the couch. "It's not just easy on the eyes — it's very comfortable, too."

My attempt to lighten the mood falls flat. Sanchez stays rooted to his spot, his lips grim.

"So," he begins, fixing his gaze on me. "I need you two to come in for questioning."

Damn! He's got something on us. Not that we weren't expecting this, but the optimist deep inside me had hoped it wouldn't come to this. Thankfully, Heather and I have discussed it in detail and have a story we both plan on sticking to.

"You're arresting us?" She joins us in the living room, looking pale.

"Not arresting you," he replies, and I fear he's barely holding back a *not yet, anyway.* "I just have a few questions for you."

"Can't you do that here?"

"It'll go a lot better at the station."

"Now?" Heather asks, her tone declaring she's not happy with this imposition.

He nods.

"Can it wait five minutes? Because I'm cooking dinner."

"Sure." A pause. "Whatever you're cooking, it smells delicious."

"Thank you." Under normal circumstances, a compliment like that would have her beaming, but she looks grim. "Or you can drive back. We'll follow as soon as we're ready."

"I'll wait."

Of course he's waiting. He can't let Heather and me huddle and discuss the situation. When she asks for five minutes, it really means fifteen. I have that math nailed down from experience. Perhaps Sanchez senses it too, because he finally tests the couch. We sit in awkward silence as he continues to peruse every visible inch of his surroundings.

Fifteen minutes later Heather steps out of the kitchen. Sanchez gets his hopes up, but she raises her finger and gives him a quick

"I'll be back" as she sprints up the stairs. That woman's not stepping out of the house without brushing her hair and applying makeup, even if it's only a doomed trip to the police station.

It's another ten minutes before she's back.

"We'll follow you in our car," she says.

"I'd rather you ride with me."

"And you'll drop us home too?" I admire her poise, because I'm trembling inside.

"Well …"

"How about this? Daniel will go with you, and I'll follow you in my car."

He stares at her.

She rewards him with a smirk. "Don't worry, Detective, I'm not going to abscond. I have two adorable children who I can't live without."

Sanchez glances at me, then turns back to Heather.

"What about your husband? Can you live without him?"

It's a strange question, considering he knows about the affair. Perhaps he assumes we've kissed and made up. Or maybe he's trying to make a point *because* he knows about it. A mischievous grin appears on her face, and I'm glad at least one of us isn't getting crushed by this situation. It's a look I was familiar with once, but one I haven't seen in a long, long time. *When did she lose that lightness of heart?*

"We've been married twenty years, Detective. What do you think?"

For my sake I hope that's a joke and she still does care about me.

Sanchez's lips almost part into a grin before tightening again.

"Let's go, then," he says.

And off we go.

27

HEATHER

A FEW WEEKS AGO

I don't hold back as I climax, unleashing loud moans on the otherwise quiet afternoon. During our previous encounters I felt inhibited, worried about what people would think if they heard me through the paper-thin motel room walls or through the flimsy door. But today I don't care, because it's the last time I'm with Patrick. At least, that's the plan.

He drops down by my side, grinning with satisfaction, beads of sweat dotting his forehead.

"You're amazing," he says as he gazes into my eyes.

I smile, because he satisfies me every single time. It's like how it used to be with Daniel in the early days. Before the kids. Before he buried himself in work. Patrick, on the other hand, is attentive and eager to please.

For a moment I wish I could turn back the clock and return to my life before Daniel fucked up the first time, a time when he couldn't get enough of me. But that's not possible, and in my state of helplessness I'm furious at Daniel. I'm raging inside like I did that night at Rancho.

"You okay?" Patrick asks. He must have noticed that my post-coital glow has melted away, replaced with something dark.

I nod. "Yeah."

I must end this today. Like I should have on our previous trysts. Today marks our fourth encounter. Yeah, I'm keeping count as my wall of shame fills up.

Why is it that the things that give us the most joy are the ones we shouldn't be indulging in? Like that frosted donut I scarfed down this morning, or the pint of ice cream I dug into last weekend, or getting fucked crazy by a handsome younger man who is not my husband. *Language, Heather.* That's probably what you want to say. Did I shock you with my choice of words? Guess what? That's the real me. A bad, bad girl trapped inside a model housewife — well, model housewife if you overlook the infidelity.

I remember the horror on Daniel's face the first time I dropped the f-bomb in his presence. It was our second date. I ensured I didn't make the same mistake again, because I adored him and I didn't want to risk losing him. And once we had kids I tried to be the perfect role model for them. Sure, they would pick up these words from their friends, but at least they wouldn't learn it from me.

Sometimes I wonder whether I made the right choice by suppressing my true self. While Daniel has been a satisfactory husband despite his flaws and indiscretions, and this marriage has given me two adorable children, would I have been happier if I'd lived my life with someone who accepted me as I am? A life where I didn't have to pretend to be a good girl. Where I didn't feel compelled to act out like I'm doing now just to feel alive. Maybe it's time to take control and get some spunk back in my life.

That day's still clear in my mind, the first time I laid eyes on Daniel. I'd walked into Plentiful Books to swipe a couple of books. Yes, swipe — bad, bad girl, remember? It's not really shoplifting if you return the goods after reading, right? *Why not use the library?* you ask. Well, I don't like secondhand copies. There's something about the fresh, crisp sensation of a new book that a used one can't match.

Anyway, so I entered the shop, and something stirred inside me when I laid eyes on Daniel. Without realizing what I was doing, I sat down for his talk, mesmerized by every word coming out of his mouth. For the first time in forever, I bought a book. It's not that I couldn't afford to buy books — it just gave me a thrill to get away with stealing them.

When I started reading *Righteous Kill*, I was riveted. I felt compelled to talk to him, get to know him. Some might say I married him for his money. They're wrong. We got together before he hit the big time, though I had no doubt, even back then, that he would scale those heights someday. Besides, I was earning considerable money myself and wanted for nothing. I married him because I loved him. Sadly, I still do.

Do I feel guilty about cheating on Daniel? For violating the sanctity of our marriage? In my weaker moments, yes. But on quiet reflection — no, not really. He beat me to it. I'm more concerned about the children. If this affair continues any longer, it's only a matter of time before someone finds out. Jonas and Joyce will be devastated. *What will they think of me?* I will have failed as a role model. As a mother. Besides, as amazing as Patrick is in bed, as much as he seems to care about me, he's immature, and I don't see this relationship — if you can call it that — going far.

I'm nervous about what I'm about to do, but I roll out of bed and start dressing. No point delaying it anymore. Patrick props himself up on his elbow, brows furrowed in concern.

"Leaving already?"

"We have to talk," I reply as I continue dressing.

He's sitting up now. "What about?"

I consider sitting next to him, but I stay put. This is the best position to deliver my message.

"This is our last time together."

He looks confused. "What? I don't understand." A pause. "Are you breaking up with me? What did I do?"

"You didn't do anything, Patrick. You've been wonderful. But this was a mistake. I'm married. I have children."

"You can leave that stuffy husband of yours. I'll take care of you and the kids."

"You don't understand. The children adore Daniel. They'll be devastated."

Patrick jumps out of bed, his face ruddy with rage. I shrink back in fear. "And you didn't know this earlier? You just used me every time you needed a fuck?"

"It's not like that. I told you — it was a mistake. I shouldn't have done this to begin with. I ... I just got carried away when I met you. But now that I'm thinking straight, I'm convinced it's not right."

"But I love you, Heather."

I freeze when I hear those words. The fool thinks he's in love with me. *What does he know about love?* We've had a bit of fun and frolic during our trysts but not much beyond that. He doesn't know the true me — what kind of person I really am behind the pleasant exterior I present to him. If he's basing this on my appearance — and I'm not sure what he sees there — how long will this infatuation last? Ten years down the road, when my face is lined and my body is sagging — will he still *love* me then? No. He'll probably move on to some pretty young thing. Whatever we have here, it's not meant to last. Now that I understand where he's coming from, I'll try to let him down nice and gentle.

"Patrick, this is not love. Let me go. Trust me on this — you'll forget about me in no time. You'll meet someone better — someone you will really, truly love. Someone who will love you back the way you deserve."

"Don't give me all this BS. I love you. I want you. We belong together."

His tone is pleading, his eyes full of pain, but I stand firm.

"No, Patrick. We don't. I'm leaving."

I turn to leave, but his next statement forces me to face him again. There's a chill in his voice now.

"Sylvia was right about you."

"Who's Sylvia?"

He bites his lip and runs his hand through his hair without responding, as if he's regretting his words. But who *is* Sylvia? I don't get a chance to probe further, because he takes a step towards me, menace emanating from his eyes. For a moment I fear he's going to hit me. "You can't leave."

Ever since we first met, I've been flattered by his intense passion for me. Now I realize, perhaps too late, that what I mistook for passion is, in reality, dangerous obsession. I dig in deeper so I can cut loose before he hurts me.

"I can, and I am. It's better we don't meet again. Goodbye."

I turn to go, but he grabs me by the arm and sticks his face close to mine. His fingers dig into my skin, his jaw clenches. "You can't do this to me, you slut!"

Shaking like a leaf, I muster enough courage to look him firmly in the eye. "Let go, Patrick. You're hurting me."

His face clears, and he releases me. "You're going to pay for this. You're going to pay."

I scurry out of the room, my relief overshadowed by the terror injected by his threat.

28

Heather

Present Day

I may have sounded calm and relaxed, cracking jokes like Sanchez was a guest we'd invited to tea, but the fact is, I was shitting bricks from the moment he showed up at our door. It took a ton of effort to not fall apart, especially after he insisted on interrogating us at the station.

It's shaping up to be a lot worse than I'd expected. On the way here I'd mentally prepared myself for the interrogation, but Sanchez sprung a nasty surprise once I arrived. He told me he wanted to fingerprint me and collect DNA. It was optional, of course — for elimination purposes — but it would help him with anything he found on Patrick or in his car. I figured it would only make me look guilty if I refused.

Sanchez departed soon after I agreed, leaving me with Officer Bennett — a pleasant old man who I would have mistaken for a retired grandpa if I'd bumped into him under different circumstances. His demeanor hasn't helped quell my nerves one bit. He has brought me over to a tech who is fingerprinting me. I go through the motions. Up next, another tech who swabs me for

DNA. All through this ordeal my heart is palpitating. I'm worried that at any moment they'll declare that I'm under arrest, and they'll humiliate me by asking me to strip naked and change into prison garb.

But those fears turn out to be unfounded, because Bennett leads me to an interrogation room and asks me to wait. It's cold, stark. Questions swirl through my mind as I sit down and he shuts the door behind him on the way out. What if I trip up during the interrogation? Should we have lawyered up? We'd discussed it, Daniel and I, long before Sanchez showed up at our doorstep. Daniel's opinion was that it would make us look guilty. If it came to it, we should proceed with the interrogation and request a lawyer only if we got backed into a corner. At that point it would make sense to zip our lips and not risk saying anything incriminating.

Time passes slowly, and eventually two hours have gone by. *What's taking so long?* I know. Sanchez must be busy grilling Daniel first before he pounces on me. All this waiting is driving me crazy. In between making a mental grocery list and trying to remember whether I moved the clothes from the washer to the dryer before I left, I've been reviewing the past few weeks of my life, my relationship with Patrick. All the mistakes I've made. If only I hadn't gotten involved with that man-child, we wouldn't be in this mess. Jonas would not have been so hurt. But what's done is done.

Yet, I'm unable to ease my guilt about the secret I've been keeping from Daniel. Another secret might not seem like a big deal, considering I still haven't told him about my days of nicking stuff from stores, and I kept my affair buried for so long. But this secret overshadows them all. Maybe someday I'll muster the nerve to come clean. That's assuming we escape this situation first.

I push those thoughts out of my head and fill it with more mundane matters. I'm deciding what to cook for lunch tomorrow when the door opens and Sanchez enters. He approaches the table and settles into the chair opposite mine.

"Where's Daniel? Did you already talk to him?"

He ignores my questions and gives me a blank stare before getting into the formalities of the interrogation. I understand this interview is being recorded, so I must be more careful about what I say.

"Patrick Delgado went missing on the eleventh. At least, that's the last time anyone saw him or heard from him. Where were you that day?"

"At home."

"Doing what?"

"The usual household stuff. Dishes. Laundry. Cooking. You know how it goes."

"And what time did Patrick get there?"

I furrow my brows to project confusion. "Patrick? He has never come to my home." Daniel and I had debated about this point. I wanted to confess that Patrick visited, but that he left once I turned him down again. Daniel felt it would complicate matters, and we should deny it outright.

"Really?"

"Yes."

"Because I know for a fact that he arrived at your house at eleven fifty-three a.m."

Of course he knows this. He has Patrick's phone records. Patrick's phone must have died some time after he arrived. Enough to show his last location to be my home.

"I clearly recall no one came to the house that day."

From the looks of it, Sanchez isn't convinced. "You sound pretty sure."

"Because I *am* sure."

"Do you always remember each day so clearly?"

It's clear where he's going with this. It's quite natural for people to not recall what happened on a particular day, so why do I remember this day so well? Unless I'm guilty and prepped my answers. He's right, of course, but I'm not going to let him in on that, am I?

"No. But I put some thought into it after you left that day."

"I see. So you're sure he didn't visit?"

"As I said before, yes, I'm sure. He has *never* visited."

A wry smile slips through Sanchez's lips. "You're lying."

"No, I'm not."

"We have plenty of evidence that proves you are."

My stomach churns. Daniel and I had anticipated the phone records. But what other information does Sanchez have?

"And what is this evidence?"

He hesitates, probably weighing whether he should reveal the source or keep his cards close to his chest.

"His phone records, for one. Location data shows he was there."

"There are other children on our street who go to the same school as my kids and are coached by Patrick. Their parents know him well, too. Maybe he came to the neighborhood to meet one of them. It doesn't prove he came to our home."

"Fair enough. But there's more."

I wait in silence while my heart and mind race — my heart because I'm terrified. My mind because it's trying to figure out what this other evidence could be. Perhaps a neighbor saw Patrick? Yes, that's probably it. Sanchez remains silent as he studies me. He's waiting too, biding his time until I break down and confess. But I'm too strong for that. At least, I like to believe so. Eventually, he caves.

"We have surveillance video showing him parking his car and entering your house."

Fuck! Fuck! Fuck! This is damning. Eric and Maisie's camera, of course. That's where he must have gotten it. For an instant I consider whether I should confess. Thankfully, that moment of weakness passes. Daniel and I had discussed our strategy in detail after Sanchez's first visit. We came up with a story and swore to stick to it, no matter what. That Sanchez would throw us curve balls was a given, but the only way to escape this mess is to stick to the plan. We were sure we would be interviewed separately — most people are aware that's how it's done. If either of us deviate from the story then Sanchez will know we're lying.

"Seriously?" I ask, trying to look as incredulous as possible without going over the top.

"Seriously," he replies calmly. He must have done this several times in his career. I'm sure he can tell I'm fibbing, but I hope I can convince him otherwise.

"Huh. I wonder how he got in." I know how he got in. Might as well offer a nugget of truth within my web of lies. "Shit! I know. I must have forgotten to lock the door again. Daniel's always after me about that."

Sanchez gives it some thought. His BS-detector must be running on overdrive. "I see. So the door's unlocked. He enters your house without your knowledge. But he stays inside for hours and you don't find out?"

"He was inside for hours?" A bolt of terror hits me as soon as I say the words, because the implications of his claim sink in. If he knows Patrick was inside our house for that long, it means Maisie's camera captured everything, including the period when we moved the body. We're doomed. The fatal flaw in our entire plan. It's all over. Sanchez already has enough to pin this on us, but he's just playing. He's hoping we'll break down and confess to make his job easier.

The children. What will happen to them if Daniel and I are arrested? If I hang for murder? Jonas will be okay. He's strong. On second thoughts — *will he be okay?*

Joyce is more sensitive. She'll take it hard. She's already devastated after Patrick's death. Losing her parents, especially in such a scandalous way, will crush her. I've always worried about her. Mothers are protective about their children, but with her even more so. Perhaps it's because I still remember Daniel's reaction when he learned I was pregnant with Joyce. That's the first time in our relationship that I resented him. He tried to hide his frustration, but it was clear he wasn't happy. Of course, he has more than made up for it by being an excellent father to her, but somewhere that moment still rankles.

"Mrs. Geraldi? Heather?"

Sanchez's firm voice pulls me back to the present. I realize my mind drifted off. That's not encouraging, since it's important I stay focused to avoid slipping up. This interrogation is critical — my life hangs in the balance. I must do everything possible to exit this dungeon looking as innocent as I was before I met Patrick.

I take a closer gander at Sanchez. He's not an attractive man, but he has the kind of personality that would make me comfortable spilling my guts if he asked nicely. His ring finger's empty, but there's a trace of something that was there before. *Did he lose his wife?* No — he would probably still be wearing the ring if that was the case. Divorce, perhaps? Does he hunger for love? If he breaks through my defenses and finds the truth, could I influence him in any way? Seduce him like those femmes fatales do in the movies? My gut tells me that won't work — he's made of sterner stuff — but it's something to keep in my back pocket for that scenario. What's the worst that could happen, anyway?

"Sorry," I reply. "What were you saying?"

"Patrick Delgado was inside your home for hours and you didn't know?"

"I seriously didn't. Maybe he hid somewhere. Maybe he was vandalizing something again."

"Did you find anything messed up? Anything out of the ordinary?"

I shake my head. "No."

"Isn't that odd?"

"I guess. Maybe it's not as obvious as the last two times," I reply, referring to the slashed tires and the graffiti. "We'll check the house once we get home." *If we get home*. Of course, I have no intention of checking.

"You do that. Wouldn't want any nasty surprises now, would we?"

His tone chills me. Clearly, this is not over yet. I give him a blank stare in response.

"Now, where was your husband that morning?"

"At a café. Writing." It's a relief to be able to sprinkle some truth here and there.

"I see. And what time did he return?"

I furrow my brows in thought again. Honestly, this act is getting tiresome. "Around twelve thirty."

"Why did he return so early?"

"What do you mean?"

"Quite early to wrap up a work day, isn't it?"

I feign offense. "It wasn't an early wrap-up. He only worked from the café for a few hours to clear his mind. The change of scenery helps trigger his creativity. The plan was to continue working out of his office once he returned."

"I see. You said the plan *was* to continue working. Did things not go according to plan?"

He doesn't miss a thing, does he? He's making it hard to keep my nerves under control.

"I didn't say that. He got home. Had lunch. And then he got back to writing."

"Now, you said he had already planned to come early. Why did you call him, then?"

The call. My distressed state. Patrick's bloody, lifeless body. It all comes back to me. I block it out before my emotions get out of hand.

"To tell him lunch was ready."

"I see."

Sanchez takes a few moments to arrange the papers in front of him. I don't think anything needs arranging. This is all for effect. Then he drills into my eyes.

"Why was he so panicked when he got home?"

The damn camera again! But would Maisie's camera capture that much detail? Perhaps this observation came from a neighbor.

"He was panicked?"

"He certainly looked it. The haphazard way he parked the car. The concern on his face as he got out. The way he hurried towards the front door."

"He was calm when I saw him."

"He was, was he?"

I nod.

"So maybe he was concerned about your well-being? He calmed down once he saw you were safe?"

"Maybe. But he never mentioned anything like that to me."

"He probably didn't want to concern you. But it sounds like Daniel was aware that you were in danger. He knew that Patrick Delgado was in your house."

"Oh," I say. "But how would he know that? And if Patrick was still in our house, where did he go?"

"That's exactly what I'd like to know."

If he has the video from Maisie's camera, he should have the answer. Is he just messing with me, or does he really not know what happened?

"Doesn't your surveillance video show you when he left?"

Sanchez is quiet for a while. It seems like he's mulling over something. Eventually he speaks.

"The problem is, the camera glitched. There's no footage for later in the day. Best I know is Delgado was in your home for four hours."

I'm surprised by his candor. It makes me wonder whether it's a ruse to catch me off guard. I would have expected him to keep his cards close to his chest and beat me into a confession. This admission that he has nothing — it's suspicious. But I'll take it. I decide to be optimistic. The moment I do that, relief surges through me. I want to laugh. I want to cry. I want to jump for joy. I want to dive into bed and sleep undisturbed for days. He hasn't seen us moving the body. Of course he hasn't. If he had, he would have already arrested us.

"I understand that you have security cameras too. We'll be heading over to your house to collect that footage."

Whatever jubilation I had experienced moments ago evaporates. I feel sick. *How did we miss that?* Our camera would have recorded everything.

"That's all I have for you at this time, Mrs. Geraldi. You're free to go."

I should be thrilled to be returning home. Instead, I'm flooded with dread, because there's no doubt I'll be arrested once Sanchez reviews the video. The walls are closing in, and I only have myself to blame.

29

ANONYMOUS

Life's a bitch. One moment you're living your life, basking in the warmth from friends and family, reaping the benefits of a successful career, and feeling blessed. Then tragedy strikes. It knocks you down and for a while you think it's all over. Until it isn't. You survive. You stagger back on your feet to fight another day. You prove to everyone that you're not down for the count. Slowly, day by day, you rebuild your life and claw back the will to live.

Then tragedy — that heartless monster — strikes again. You're flat on your back once more, wondering how some fortunate people sail through life not knowing what hardship is, how grief breaks you down every single day. *Why me?* you ask. But, once again, you pick yourself up. You find a purpose in life, anything that will help you sail through the days.

So, fighter that I am, I take a pledge. I will soldier on. I will march down the path I've set for myself until I've attained my goals.

30

DANIEL

I've described police interrogation rooms in some of my novels, but this is the first time I've been inside one. It's quite an experience so far. The stark environment, the feeling of claustrophobia. Everything designed to make me uncomfortable. Over the rising dread within me, I take in the details. If I ever make it out of here, it will help me describe it better the next time around.

Even the fingerprinting and the DNA collection was an experience. Sanchez just sprang that on me. I thought we were here for an interrogation only, but he's a smart cookie, that one. I didn't see any reason to decline. We've taken precautions, and I'm confident the cops won't find a match that will link me to Patrick's death. Refusal, on the other hand, could be detrimental to our prospects.

It doesn't take long for Sanchez to show up in the room. He strides over to the table and settles into the chair opposite mine, placing a folder bulging with sheets of paper on the table and staring at it. I wonder about Heather. Is she seated in a room similar to this one? Is someone interrogating her right now, or will she have

to wait for Sanchez to finish with me? And most importantly —
will she stick to the plan?

"Daniel, where were you on the eleventh?" Sanchez's voice
shakes me out of my thoughts. He's looking at me now.

"The eleventh? The day Patrick Delgado went missing?"

"Yes."

"I was writing at a café that morning."

"Is that something you do often?"

"Writing? Yes, that's how I make a living."

Sanchez winces, clearly not appreciating my sense of humor.
Honestly, I've surprised myself by saying that, given my dire situation.

"Writing at cafés? Yes, occasionally. It gets too monotonous
staying cooped up in my office."

"I see. And how long did you stay there that day?"

"I left close to noon, I think. Went straight home."

"And why did you leave?"

Stick to the plan. Stick to the plan, I remind myself.

"Heather wanted me home for lunch."

"You had discussed this before you left home in the morning?"

"Kinda. But she called to confirm. That's when I headed back."

Sanchez pauses and stares at the folder again, his fingers grazing
its edges. When he looks up at me again with his cold eyes, I know
the soft questions are over. He's going on the offensive. I brace for
impact, not sure what grenades he's going to lob at me next.

"Daniel, if this was just a routine return, why were you so panicked when you got there?"

And there it is. I'm guessing he got that from a neighbor. Rhonda, perhaps? I feign confusion. "Panicked? I don't remember being panicked."

"That's not what I saw. The rushed way you parked your car, your hurried footsteps towards the door, the concern on your face — it all tells me something was up."

He *saw?* Ah, this must be from Maisie's camera. My belly flutters as I kick myself for not thinking of that. This one mistake could sink our boat. If her camera caught me coming home, it would have captured Heather and me disposing of the body. I'm sweating now and finding it hard to breathe, but I wipe my hands on my jeans and compose myself. This won't end well if I falter and don't respond.

"I'd have remembered if I was panicked. I wasn't. If I recall correctly, I needed to pee ... real bad." I shrug. "Coffee, you know."

Sanchez smiles. A genuine smile of amusement. I had no idea he was capable of that.

"Okay, so you weren't panicked. I'll take that. Were you aware that Patrick Delgado was inside your house?"

"He was?" I think I'm faking surprise quite well, though I can't tell whether he's buying it.

"Yes, he was. You must have seen his car outside."

"I don't know what he drives." A pause. "Was it something flashy?"

"No. Just a regular Accord. Why do you think it would be flashy?"

"Because you expected me to notice it."

"Ah, right." He adjusts his folder again before continuing. "Tell me what happened when you went inside."

"Heather had just finished cooking. The place smelled divine. I peed and then we sat down for lunch."

"What did you eat?"

We skipped lunch that day. Patrick kept us busy. Of course, I can't share that nugget with Sanchez. I plaster on a smile before replying.

"I barely remember what I ate yesterday. No idea what we had that day."

"But you remember the divine smell. What did you smell, Daniel?"

I don't like where this is going, but I maintain the smile. "Sorry, I can't help you there. I just remember that whatever it was, it was good."

"Okay. What happened next?"

"Well, we ate. We talked. Then I snuck into my office to continue writing."

Sanchez leans forward, his eyes boring into mine.

"So you never suspected someone was inside your house?"

"No. Not at all. It was like any other day."

"Daniel, I know for a fact that Patrick Delgado was inside your house that afternoon."

"Really?" My heart is hammering now.

"Yes. Perhaps he was there for — how do I put this delicately — for another tryst with your wife, and he was forced to hide when you returned."

I frown. "That doesn't make any sense. Why would Heather call me home if she was meeting him there?"

"Maybe she didn't know he was coming."

"That's possible. But why would she want to be with him after all that awful stuff he did to us?"

"I don't know. Maybe they patched things up. Now, I completely understand it if you got home, found them together, and killed Patrick in a jealous rage."

I grit my teeth, trying to look offended. "Nothing of the sort happened. I already told you — I did not see him that day." And it's the truth, well most of it — I didn't kill the sleazeball, though I did see him.

"Okay, so let's assume you didn't see him. But he did step inside your house — before you arrived. And he didn't leave for a long time."

"How long?"

"A few hours at least."

"You don't know for sure?"

Sanchez hesitates. I'm desperate to learn what he knows. The fact that Heather and I are here tells me he suspects us, but my gut convinces me he doesn't have anything concrete on us, because if he did, he would have already arrested us. There's still hope that our plan leads us to freedom.

"I noticed you have security cameras outside your house."

So he has decided not to give me details. He's still keeping his cards close to his chest. *Why is he interested in my cameras? Did he not get enough footage from Maisie's?*

"Yes, I do."

"And they work?"

"Yes."

"I need to review the recordings from that day."

I frown. "Don't you already have footage from some other camera? The same one on which you saw me entering the house."

"I need more."

"I doubt you'll get anything."

"Why is that?"

"It's set to retain the videos for two days only."

I'm breathing much easier now, complimenting myself for this stroke of genius. I may have goofed by not remembering Maisie's camera, but I sure didn't forget mine. Last night I deleted all the recordings older than two days, and I changed the settings to retain videos from one week to two days. I forgot to tell Heather about this.

"I still want to check."

He doesn't trust me. Of course, he doesn't. I wouldn't trust me if I were in his shoes.

"Sure. Whatever you need." I'm the model of cooperation, aren't I?

He extends his hand.

"Your phone."

"What do you need my phone for?"

"Don't you have an app for the camera?"

"I do, but my phone's dead. We'll have to go home and check it on my laptop."

He can't hide his disappointment, and I delight in it. Of course, I'm careful not to show it.

"Alright. Let's go, then."

He stands up. It takes me a moment to realize the interview is over. Lightness descends on me. I'm home free! But our fate still hangs in the balance, because it depends on how Heather fares in her interview.

We exit the room and walk down the corridor. Sanchez stops to speak to a jolly-looking cop, who I learn is Officer Bennett. Sanchez is speaking softly, so soft that I'm unable to catch most of the conversation. Bennett turns to me with a stern look, drained of all the jolly.

"Let's go," he says as Sanchez heads back down towards the interrogation room.

Bennett leads me to the parking lot where he directs me to enter the rear of a patrol car, while he gets in the driver's seat. I wonder why Sanchez isn't coming himself. Perhaps he has gone back to interview Heather?

Bennett drives off. As with the interrogation room, I've never been inside a patrol car, so I take in the details the best I can. It's information I can use in some future novel. Assuming I don't earn a criminal record thanks to my current predicament. In which case I might end up penning a memoir titled *My Life Behind Bars*.

A short ride later we approach my street, and my body tens-es. I feel like a common criminal, dreading what the neighbors will think when they see me stepping out from the rear of a black-and-white. Thankfully I'm not handcuffed, but the general imagery doesn't work in my favor. My mood sours further since handcuffs remind me of my ordeal in Sacramento.

As we turn onto our street, I scan my surroundings. Not a soul in sight, and it raises my spirits. But as Bennett slows down outside my house, I spot Maisie and Killian playing in their front yard. She stops to observe us. My face is burning in embarrassment as I exit the car. She doesn't smile or wave, maintaining a neutral demeanor. But Killian's face erupts into glee as he waves and says, "Hi, Daniel" in his cute voice. He enjoys my company, and me his, though I suspect his liking me has more to do with the fact that he's a fan of *Daniel Tiger* and I happen to have the same name.

I wave back and turn towards my house. Rhonda's peeking through her front window. This is trouble. If she has seen this, then soon the entire street will know about it.

Bennett and I enter the house. I lead him to my office and launch the camera website on the laptop just like Jonas taught me. He settles into the chair to review the footage.

"Would you like something, Officer? Coffee? Water?"

He shakes his head, focusing on the screen. I wait patiently for him to finish, trying not to imagine Heather messing up her interview and landing us behind bars.

"Yeah, there's nothing here," he says finally, confirming what I know, and what I told Sanchez. In spite of everything, I'm relieved, as if there was a chance those incriminating videos would have reappeared.

"That's what I told Sanchez," I reply.

"Doesn't hurt to check. I guess my work here's done." He stands. "Enjoy the rest of your day. I'll find my way out."

And just like that, Bennett's gone. I slump into my chair and let out a breath. I'm exhausted. I should catch up on sleep. Or eat something — it's been a while since I did, but all I can think of is Maisie and her videos. I know it's the wrong thing to do, but I march out, heading straight for the house across the street. The moment Maisie spots me, she grabs Killian and rushes inside, shutting the door. Though I started running as soon as she made her move, I'm too late. Not surprising, considering my poor fitness level. I attack her doorbell first, and when that doesn't work, I start banging on her door.

The door opens a minute later to reveal Eric standing there. He looks grumpy. Can't blame him, can I?

"What do you want, Daniel?"

"It was you, wasn't it? You shared videos from your camera with Sanchez."

"We didn't have a choice. He showed up at our door and asked if he could review the footage. We just wanted to help the law, like any responsible citizen would."

He's right. I don't know why I'm so angry at him and Maisie. I guess I'm just frustrated with everything that's going on, and part of the reason I'm in this mess is because of his videos. It's easy to vent my frustration on him.

"Did you have anything to do with that guy's death?" he asks.

"No, of course not! How can you even think that?"

"I'm sorry. It's just that, from what I understand, he was last seen entering your house."

"Yes, that's what I've been told. But if I had something to do with it, they wouldn't let me go, would they?"

He considers my response for a bit. "I don't know. It's not like they know how he got from your house to the park."

"Your videos would have shown him leaving, though, right?"

"See, that's the problem. The camera glitched again that evening. There's no footage. The last thing we see is his car still parked outside, and no one entering or leaving after you arrived."

This is why we're safe. No one has seen us disposing of Patrick. It's ironic that only recently I was disappointed that the glitches resulted in us not knowing who was vandalizing our cars. Now the same glitches have saved us. My body relaxes. Perhaps we will make it out of this hole after all. I thank Eric and return to my house. All I can do now is wait for Heather, keeping my fingers crossed that she aces her interview like I aced mine.

31

DANIEL

I'm out for a walk around the block, getting some fresh air and exercise in an effort to clear my mind. It's a beautiful day, with cloudless blue skies and the sun taking it easy on us mortals for a change. With no further incidents, it seems Pen or whoever was after me is lying low. It has allowed me to be more relaxed and not treat every movement in the neighborhood with suspicion. My stress about the Patrick investigation is also dying down, though we could still land in trouble if Sanchez finds fresh evidence.

As I approach my house at the end of the second lap, eager to escape inside and draft the next chapter in Fiona's saga, I see Rhonda standing outside her house. As usual, she's in running gear, and from the look of it, she has already knocked off her daily six miles. And here I am, content that I strolled for a few minutes. It reminds me that back in Sac I'd promised myself to start running soon. Tomorrow, for sure.

"Hi, Daniel," she says when I'm close enough.

"Hi, Rhonda."

I brace for impact, concerned that she's going to unleash a scathing review of one of my novels.

"We need to talk." Her voice has dropped to a whisper, and she's throwing furtive glances around.

"About what?"

"Not here. Come inside."

"Inside your home?" I can't believe she's inviting me into her home.

"Of course, Daniel. Where else?" she replies, exasperated like a parent whose child just asked the same question the hundredth time.

I've never been alone with her indoors. Now, I'm not a prude or anything, but Heather seemed suspicious the last time I spoke to Rhonda on the street. I can only imagine her reaction when she finds out I was alone with our neighbor behind closed doors.

"Do we have to?" I ask.

"What I want to say can't be shared out in the open. I think you'll appreciate it once I tell you what it's about."

I hesitate, but I'm curious enough to follow her inside. Bruno comes bounding towards us as soon as we enter, and for a moment I fear for my life. Has Rhonda lured me in so he can attack me and exact revenge for what I did? It's a silly thought, and I dismiss it immediately. He gets real close, and a lesser fear emerges. Is he going to lick my hand? Thankfully, he knows better. He nuzzles Rhonda's hand and accompanies her to the living room. Once there, she plops down onto the couch and motions me to sit on the chair opposite. Bruno sits by her side, tongue hanging out of his mouth as he glares at me. I stare back at him and his hair. He probably sheds a lot. The thought makes me feel icky, wondering whether I'm sitting on dog hair right now. My imagination runs wild and I shudder, picturing myself drowning in dog hair. A terrible way to die.

"So, I read *Righteous Kill*." A faint smile plays on Rhonda's lips.

Surely that's not what she invited me in here for, but now I'm curious. I wait with bated breath for her to tell me it sucked.

"I actually liked it. Pretty good for a debut novel. I can't wait to devour the rest of your books."

"Whew! That's a relief." And relieved I am, but it doesn't take long for the doubt to creep in. What if she's using the sandwich method here, and this positive feedback is a lead-in to the terrible news she's about to deliver?

We sit in silence for a few seconds. The calm before the storm, I sense. When she speaks, it's beyond my worst nightmares.

"I saw you, you know."

"Saw me? What do you mean?"

"You and Heather with that man's body. Patrick Delgado."

And there it is. A solid punch to my gut that sends me reeling. My heart starts pounding. I break into a sweat. This can't be. This can't be.

"I saw you rolling up his body and cleaning up the mess."

"How ... how did you?" I blurt out without thinking. *Imbecile!* I curse myself. The least I could do is deny it.

"From your side window. I couldn't resist checking up on you after you rushed in in panic mode."

Damn peeping Tom! I want to lash out at her for being such a snoop, but that would just aggravate the situation.

"Have you … have you told anyone?"

"Not yet."

"What do you want?" She could have told the cops. If she hasn't, I expect she wants to blackmail me.

She looks amused. "You think I'm going to extort you?"

"Well, isn't that … isn't that how this works?" My mouth is so dry, I can hardly get the words out.

"Seriously, Daniel. Look around you." Her eyes sweep the surroundings, her hand following in sync. "Do you think I need money? I'm a forty-five-year-old single woman with a flourishing career that pays me well. No kids, no dependents. Except Bruno, of course. I have more money than I know what to do with."

As if drowning in riches has ever stopped people from coveting more. Human greed is what it is.

"Then why are you telling me this?"

"Because I've known you guys for so long, and in spite of your quirks, I think you are decent folks. I want to give you a chance to explain what happened."

Hmm … this is just as unexpected as her revelation. She can't be that stupid, can she? If she thinks we killed Patrick, then why risk being alone with me? Isn't she concerned I might murder her too?

"Now, if you're thinking of killing me, let me stop you right there." It's as if she read my mind. "At least one neighbor saw us walking in together. If something happens to me, you'll be the prime suspect."

Okay, so she's not stupid. I should have figured. Now I'm curious about this neighbor. Is this the same one as Heather's "source"?

"So, do you have something to say for yourself?"

"I do. But before I begin. Why me? Why not talk to Heather?" That would make sense, given our frosty relationship and the fact that she's on friendly terms with my beloved.

"Because I enjoy seeing you squirm, Daniel."

God, I want to wipe that smirk off her face!

I realize I've been squirming ever since she dropped the bombshell. There'll be less of that now so I can deny her the pleasure. I tell her the story. She listens intently, except for one interruption where she expresses shock about Heather's affair. *Yeah, that surprised me too, lady.* She's quiet for a while once I have finished.

"What he did was awful, but he didn't deserve to die."

"I agree. But like I said, it was an accident."

"Which you covered up." There's no trace of any smile or smirk on her face anymore. Her stern gaze would intimidate anybody. "I'm not okay with that."

"I understand. It wasn't our best moment. We panicked." I let my reply sink in before continuing. "So, what are you going to do?"

"I'll be talking to the cops."

No! No, no, no!

"Please, Rhonda. We have children to take care of. Think about what will happen to them if we go to prison."

"You should have thought of that before crossing the line."

I wish I hadn't gone along with Heather. We should have called 911 that day. At least then she would have gone free eventually, and I wouldn't be in any sort of trouble either. Now we're both toast.

"Can you give us some time?"

"Time? Time for what? You've already enjoyed a few extra days of freedom. Honestly, I've been debating about this, or I would have reported you that very day."

"Time that we can spend as a family. This will be our last chance before we're arrested."

She chews on my request for a bit.

"Two days. That's the best I can do."

"Thank you, Rhonda. I really appreciate that."

"But there's a catch." Her smug countenance is nauseating. "You have to do something for me."

"What?"

"Come here and pet Bruno."

So vengeful. So spiteful. *How about I come over and squeeze your throat instead, you sorry excuse for a woman?* I don't want to touch Bruno, but do I have a choice? I suppress my urge to throttle her, because I don't consider myself a violent man. The temptation worries me, though. I grew up in a home where physical abuse was a frequent occurrence, and I've been at the receiving end, too. That kind of an environment can scar a person, especially one at an impressionable age as I was back then. *Do I have a predilection for violence like my father did?* I'd like to believe I don't, but now I'm not so sure. There must be better ways to deal with this woman. Heather and I will come up with something.

"Come on, Daniel. I haven't got all day. If we spend any more time alone in here, the neighbors will gossip."

I get off the chair and glance at Bruno. His ears perk up as he stares at me. I take a few steps towards him and he flinches, probably remembering our regrettable encounter.

"It's okay, Bruno." Rhonda places a hand on his head.

He calms down. She takes her hand off, and I place mine on. I stroke his fur gently. It's soothing, if I stop thinking about how I must sanitize my hand once I'm out of here. This sensation reminds me of when Jonas and Joyce were babies. Those days and nights when they rested their little heads on my chest, me stroking their soft hair and my hand grazing their smooth skin. Pure bliss — the bright spots in those dark, stressful, sleep-deprived periods of my life.

Bruno makes the most of this opportunity to resurrect our friendship by licking my hand. I draw away, but Rhonda's raised eyebrow forces my hand back. I try to ignore the icky feeling as he satisfies his urges.

"That's good enough," Rhonda says after what seems like eons.

I withdraw my hand in an instant.

She stands up and looks me in the eye. "Two days, Daniel. Two days. You may go now."

Having been dismissed, I turn to leave, but a thought crosses my mind. It's a question that's been nagging me for a while. I've suppressed it all this time, not wanting to jeopardize my relationship with my neighbor, but now there's not much left to salvage anyway. So I spin around and confront her.

"That night a few months ago — you were spying on me and Heather through our living room window, weren't you?"

Her face turns red. It's a few beats before she speaks. "I wasn't spying, Daniel. I thought I heard a scream."

"A scream? Coming from our house?"

"Yes. I was worried about Heather."

For a moment I'm confused, but her face tells me what's going on in her crazy head.

"You thought I'd hurt her?"

She nods. *The nerve of this woman!*

"For the record, I've never laid a finger on her. And never will. Why would you even think such a thing?"

"Because I wonder what a nice woman like her is doing with a self-obsessed prick like you."

"I'm not—"

Rhonda cuts me off by raising her hand.

"Don't get me wrong — I know you love your wife and kids, but you're still selfish enough to put your needs above theirs."

"What makes you think—"

The commanding hand again.

"If you think I'm so terrible, why are you reading my books, huh?"

"To understand you better, Daniel. I'm sure the ugliness within you spills into your writing. Honestly, from what I've read so far, you're a sick, sick person."

I open my mouth to speak again, but The Empress dismisses me with a wave of her hand, escalating my hatred for her to new heights. I trudge back home, shaking inside, wondering how I'm going to wriggle out of this predicament.

32

DANIEL

"She said what?" Heather looks as shocked as I was when Rhonda told me. She's pacing about the room. The last time I saw her this agitated was when she came clean about the affair. At the time I'd thought it was the low point of my life, but this situation is a million times worse.

"We have two days. That's it."

"The nerve of that woman! Peeking through our windows all the time."

"What do we do about it?"

She stops pacing and locks eyes with me. "I'll talk to her."

"I doubt that will help. She has made up her mind."

"Still got to give it a shot, Daniel. We can't cave so easily when our lives are at stake." Her hands are on her waist now. Under normal circumstances I'd rib her about her Wonder Woman stance, but I'm too devastated to comment.

"Okay, but we still need a plan B."

"Which is?"

"Which is what we have to figure out."

"Well, you figure it out, then. I'll go talk to that ... woman."

Heather storms out of the room, leaving me alone with my thoughts ... and the feeling that I'm going to be sick any moment. I settle on the couch and mull over the problem, but every path leads to the same disconcerting conclusion — Rhonda must die. I pray fervently that Heather is able to convince her, for Rhonda's own sake. But since we need a plan B, I travel deeper down the dark route.

I've formulated a half-baked plan by the time Heather returns, looking deflated. She shakes her head when she sees me.

"She didn't budge?" I ask.

"No. I wanted to strangle her right there, Bruno be damned."

Even in these dire circumstances I muster a chuckle. "Exactly my thoughts when she told me."

"But you didn't do it."

I raise an eyebrow. "You really think I could do that?"

She studies my face for a moment before replying. "No."

I find the meek, delayed response concerning.

"You didn't do it either," I say.

"That shouldn't surprise you," she snaps back.

I nod. "No, it doesn't." A pause. "But we have to do something about her. We need a plan B."

She's seated by my side now, her hopeful eyes boring into mine. "Did you come up with anything?"

"She has to go, Heather. There's no other way."

Her lip quivers. "And by go you mean ..."

"You know what I mean. We have to kill her."

Heather springs up from the couch. "No! No way, Daniel. We can't."

"What alternative do we have?"

"I don't know. Come up with something. You're the creative one."

"Heather ..."

But it's futile, because she storms out of the room again. I'm glued to the couch for a long time, weighing all our options once again. Try as I might, only that one option stands out. So I bake my plan further until it's ready. They say poison is a woman's weapon. I counter that it's a smart person's weapon. Especially a smart person like me who despises violence.

Rhonda gave us two days. If things go as planned, she won't wake up to see that second day.

33

DETECTIVE SANCHEZ

Sanchez is at his desk, deep in thought. The interviews didn't go well. Not well at all. He had hoped one of the Geraldis would slip up, and he would be able to force a confession, but they outwitted him. They were both lying, he's sure of it. His sharp instincts and rich experience can't be wrong. Their success shouldn't surprise him, though. Daniel Geraldi spins yarns for a living, and crime stories at that. He's pretty good at it, from the looks of it. Heather Geraldi's been screwing another man behind her husband's back. That requires some guile. Definitely a woman adept at dissembling — not one to be trusted. But still, he had hoped this would be different. Knowing you're suspected of murder — stewing in an interrogation room and getting grilled by a detective — that would rattle anyone. But those two handled it remarkably well.

And now Bennett tells him there's no video from the Geraldis' camera. *Fuck!* Sanchez knows he has goofed. He should have grabbed the footage as soon as he got the location data. Instead, he collected the videos from the O'Donnells, which, though helpful, aren't as substantial as what he could have got from the Geraldis. Some sloppy detective work right there.

How will he face Patrick's sister now? She demanded he find the killer, and he assured her that he would. What can he do to make it happen?

His mind wanders to the interview with Heather — a beauty. Under different circumstances — if she wasn't a suspect, if she wasn't married, if she wasn't a cheat — he would have asked her out. In fact, in spite of everything, part of him *wants* to ask her out. She's way out of his league, of course, and he could never muster the courage anyway. Sanchez stares at his empty ring finger, the faint trace of his wedding band still visible. It's at times like this that he misses Trish. *How did he end up like this — like a clichéd detective from the movies?* Working long hours, drinking too much, to the point where Trish couldn't take it anymore and had no choice but to walk away. He has cleaned up his act since, but it's too late now. Trish has moved on. He should start dating again. Or at least get laid to take the edge off.

He realizes his thoughts are straying. He should be focusing on the investigation. Heather's not a killer. He's sure of it. *Or is he too infatuated with her to think straight?* Daniel, on the other hand, has it in him to take a life. It's what Sanchez's instincts tell him. If that's the case, then she's probably lying to protect her husband. Can't blame her. Maybe she still loves him. Maybe she thinks it's the least she can do to atone after cheating on him.

All this thinking, and what does Sanchez have to show for it? Nothing. It's not often that he's stumped about his next move.

Perhaps he'll turn in early tonight and sleep on it. Sometimes the best ideas manifest themselves in his dreams.

34

DANIEL

It's early evening when I hear barking from Rhonda's. I've rarely heard Bruno bark, though. Five, ten minutes go by, but he doesn't stop.

"Is that Bruno?" Joyce asks as she enters the living room, followed by Jonas.

"Sure sounds like him," Heather replies, emerging from the kitchen. "I wonder what's wrong." She pauses before adding, "Can one of you help me lay the table?"

Joyce volunteers, and soon we're settled at the table for dinner. Heather has prepared light fare tonight — cranberry walnut chicken salad and roasted vegetable sandwiches. We dig in and try to make conversation, but the barks make it difficult to enjoy the meal.

"Poor thing. I hope he's okay," Joyce says in between bites of her sandwich.

"I would be more worried about Rhonda." Jonas stabs a slice of chicken. "Bruno wouldn't be barking if she was home watching him. Maybe she's in some kind of trouble."

Heather and I glance at each other. She looks concerned. We didn't discuss plan B after our last exchange. She knew we only had one option, but she didn't want to hear anymore about it. Any knowledge of my scheme would make it too real for her, and she's not ready to handle something like that after the Patrick fiasco.

"I'll check on her as soon as we're done," she says. "Joyce, Jonas, please help clear the table while I'm gone."

"On it, Captain," Jonas replies with a military salute. Joyce rolls her eyes. At least it helps put a smile on Heather's face, though her eyes betray the turmoil within. I don't feel too good myself. Guilt is tearing me apart, and I fear what they will find inside Rhonda's home. The suspense is unbearable.

Heather leaves after a few minutes. The children return to their rooms after completing their chores. I try to watch a movie on Netflix to drown out the barking, but I can't focus. I stare at our new coffee table, picturing the old one in its place, with Patrick's lifeless body on top. Blood everywhere. Somehow that image is comforting compared to seeing Rhonda dead. At least I wasn't responsible for the former.

I turn off the TV when Heather returns, eagerly waiting for her update. She takes her time, settling into the loveseat instead of next to me on the couch.

"She didn't answer. I knocked several times. Tried the doorbell several times, but no response. Bruno even ran up to the door and barked. Poor thing. Some of the other neighbors joined in. We called 911. Someone is on the way."

I remain silent, not knowing what to say, hoping she can't hear my thudding heart.

"Her car's not in the driveway," Heather says.

"Maybe she parked it in the garage?"

"You know she never does that. There's no room with all the junk she's got in there."

Which means Rhonda's not at home. It doesn't make sense. Unless …

I don't want to think about it. No point speculating. The cops will be here soon, and we'll know exactly where she is and what happened to her. The thought makes me want to throw up.

As if on cue, red and blue lights flash outside. We step into the cool evening air, and it helps a bit with the nausea once I remind myself to breathe. An officer exits the police cruiser and walks up the driveway towards Rhonda's home. Some of the other neighbors congregate.

He raises his hand. "I'm Officer Howard. Who called it in?"

Laurie steps forward from the cluster of neighbors and walks over to Howard. "I did." She lives two houses down, across the street. She and Rhonda were close. Is she the one who Rhonda claimed saw me enter her house that day? Hopefully no one witnessed me enter or exit the last time I was in there. I was careful, but one never knows.

Laurie and Howard have a brief conversation where she explains the situation. He turns around and tries the doorbell a few times. Then he knocks. Bruno's been barking all this time. When there's no response, Howard walks along the periphery of the structure, trying to peek in through every window that's not covered in curtains or blinds. From the change in the barks, it sounds like Bruno's following him.

Having exhausted all avenues, Howard addresses us. "So, here's the thing. Normally in a situation like this, I would have entered the house to check if she's okay. But as I've been told, her car is not here. Quite likely she's not inside. Maybe she went to work and got held up with something. She might turn up soon."

"This has never happened before, Officer," Laurie says. "Not once in all the years she has lived here. And I've been trying her phone all day. It goes straight to voicemail."

"But that doesn't mean she's in there. If something happened to her, it happened where she went."

"We still need to help Bruno. Her dog." She pauses, then adds, "I have a spare key."

Howard furrows his brows. "Why do you have a key to her house?"

Laurie looks offended, as if he'd accused her of something. "Rhonda travels a lot for work. She gave it to me so I could take care of Bruno and water the plants whenever she's away."

"I see. Why didn't you use it this time?"

"I ... I was worried about what I would find in there."

"Do you have it with you right now?"

She nods and hands him the key.

"Wait here." He turns towards the front door, opens it, and steps inside. Bruno's barks grow louder before fading.

My heart's been pounding all this time, and I have to remind myself to breathe again. The moment of truth is approaching. I'm like the hunter who sets a trap and walks away, not knowing whether any animal took the bait and landed in there.

"Did you try calling her?" I ask Heather while we wait.

"I didn't see the point."

"What do you mean?"

"You know what I mean." Her response is cold, emotionless. For some reason, it strikes terror inside me. Does she have something to do with whatever happened to Rhonda? What if I have it all wrong and Heather plotted and executed a plan B by herself? A few weeks ago such a doubt would not have entered my mind. But now I'm not sure whether I really know my wife. If she can be brazen enough to cheat on me, she can take a life if the need arises.

"She's not in there." Howard steps out with a calm Bruno by his side.

I'm disappointed. That's how callous a person I have become. The fact is, I was hoping Howard would find Rhonda dead so that I would know Heather and I were safe. Now there's still a chance she's alive and well, and she'll tell the cops about what we did to Patrick.

"So what's next, Officer?" Laurie asks.

"Nothing, at this point. It's been less than twenty-four hours since she's been gone. We have to give it another day or two before we consider her missing and take action."

"But I'm telling you, something's wrong. If she's not home yet and she's not answering her phone, it means she's in trouble."

"I understand, but we have to wait." He glances at Bruno. "Now, about the dog."

"I can watch him," she offers.

"Thank you," Officer Howard replies before leaving in his cruiser.

The excitement for the day over, everyone turns towards their homes. Heather and I return to ours. I want to talk to her, clear the air about this situation, but I sense she's not in the mood, and I dare not poke the beast. It's as if by ignoring it she makes the problem go away. So I stay quiet.

35

DETECTIVE SANCHEZ

A few days have passed, but Sanchez doesn't have any break-throughs in the case. The only prints inside Patrick's car were his own. There was no trace of Daniel's DNA in there. He had hoped there would be a match, but alas. Two strands of blonde hair in the center console and on the driver's seat raised his hopes for a bit — Heather's hair, he's certain — but she could easily explain that away. Patrick and she had been lovers after all, and it wouldn't be unusual for her to have been in his car.

Today Sanchez received a new lead, from Patrick's sister no less. Unfortunately, it meant she was furious at him for the lack of progress. *How come she had unearthed this nugget, but Sanchez and his incompetent team had come up with nothing?* she had asked. He and his team are not incompetent. Certainly not, if you ignore the one lapse with the videos from the Geraldis' camera. But he has to concede that she has a point. How did they miss this key information?

He heads over to the home of the Aroras — Rishi and Mita. They're neighbors of the Geraldis, and he's been told that Mita saw them disposing of the body. Sylvia Delgado canvassed the entire neighborhood and came up with this treasure. She took the initiative because she was convinced the cops weren't doing their jobs, that they were twiddling their thumbs, with their feet on their desks, downing piña coladas while Patrick's killer roamed free. So untrue. They've been working hard, but sometimes hard work is not enough. Even smarts aren't enough. Sometimes you need those lucky breaks. He hopes this is one such break.

Sanchez parks outside the Arora residence. It's two houses away from the Geraldis. Close enough to notice someone hauling a corpse. He strides up to the front door. A picture of Ganesha rests above the peephole. Sanchez knows his Hindu deities because at one point Trish had developed a strong interest in Hinduism. It was only later that he found out that the guy she was seeing — and the one she moved on with — was a Hindu.

He knocks, finding a spot that doesn't disturb the ele-phant-headed god. The door opens to reveal a petite woman standing there.

"You must be Detective Sanchez," she says in a lilting voice.

"And you must be Mita."

"Guilty as charged." She giggles and waits for a beat. "Sorry, couldn't resist that. Come on in."

Sanchez ekes out a smile. It is kinda funny — punny, even — he has to admit. But he's trying to maintain a professional demeanor. It's a murder investigation, after all. He follows her through the passage to the living room. The floor plan is the same as the

Geraldis', he observes. Interesting how the same layout is furnished differently.

A man steps out of the kitchen and extends his hand. "Rishi Arora," he says with a firm handshake. "Please sit." He gestures towards the seating area.

Sanchez settles into the couch, and Mita sits on one of the chairs opposite.

"Try some Indian sweets." Rishi offers a box to him. "We just got back from a long trip to India a few days ago."

That explains it, Sanchez realizes. That's how they missed the Aroras during canvassing. The family wasn't home. He glances at the box, full of diamond-shaped pieces, calculating how many extra minutes on the treadmill each morsel will cost him. He really shouldn't indulge.

"No, thank you," he replies.

"A piece or two won't hurt. Unless you have a nut allergy. It's made with cashew nuts."

Sanchez picks up a piece. "Thank you." He takes a bite. Not bad. Not bad at all. He puts the rest of it in his mouth, relishing every bit.

"Would you like some tea?" Rishi again.

Sanchez has tried Indian tea at the restaurant across the street from his apartment. Too sweet. The food was delicious, though.

"No, thank you."

Rishi places the box on the coffee table and joins Mita on the chair next to hers. Sanchez is relieved, because he's eager to begin the interview.

"Rishi, Mita, thank you for meeting with me today. As I mentioned over the phone, this is regarding the death of Patrick Delgado."

"Very sad," Mita says, shaking her head.

"Tragic," adds Rishi.

"Did you know him well?"

"I wouldn't say that. Just a little chat here and there when dropping and picking up our daughter from soccer class. Anya loved him. It's been a shock for her," Mita replies.

"That's understandable. Was she in the same class as Joyce Geraldi?"

"Yes. Joyce and Anya are close."

"Patrick's sister, Sylvia, told me you saw something the night he disappeared. The eleventh of last month."

"Yes, she was over here a couple of days ago, asking about that day."

"And?"

"I'd stepped out of the house for some fresh air that night. As soon as I got out, I saw Daniel and Heather carrying something to their minivan."

"What time was this?"

"Around midnight, I think."

Sanchez raises his eyebrow. "That late?"

"Yes. I was up packing for our trip to India."

"I see. What were they carrying?"

"It looked like a rolled-up rug."

"You sure about that?"

Mita considers the question. "Well, it was dark. Plus, I was pre-occupied, since we were flying the next morning. And there was the whole drama with Anya's passport. I only saw a bit, as much as I could make out in the dark. I didn't think much of it at the time, but when she — Sylvia — asked about it, I figured it could be relevant."

"So you saw them carry out a rug to their car. Anything else?"

"They brought out some trash bags as well."

"What did they do after that?"

"They went back inside. I don't know what happened after that, because I returned inside."

"How about you, Rishi? Did you see or hear anything suspicious?"

Rishi shakes his head. "Nothing. Sorry."

Well, that's not much to go on, thinks Sanchez. Sure, it does indicate that the Geraldis might have moved Patrick's body in the dead of the night, but there's no concrete evidence. Nothing that he can move on. If only the O'Donnells' camera hadn't glitched. If only Sanchez had been smart enough to review the videos from the Geraldis earlier. At the very least he should have secured a warrant and searched their home as soon as he knew that was where Patrick visited last. Their empty living room should have told him something was up — that that's where Patrick probably breathed his last. Now the Geraldis are already on high alert, and if they'd missed any cleanup earlier, they must have taken care of it by now. Mistakes. Blunders. Regrets. Plenty of those in Sanchez's life.

"Thank you for your time." He stands, shrugging off the disappointment that's weighing him down. He offers them his card. "Call me if you remember anything else."

"Sure," says Rishi as he takes the card and inspects it. "You really think they did it? Murdered Patrick, I mean?"

"Can't say. Just checking out every angle, that's all."

With that, Sanchez turns and leaves, wondering whether he will ever catch a break in this case.

36

DANIEL

Rhonda was training for a full marathon a couple of years ago. We were excited for her at first, rooting for her as she trained, marveling at her drive for taking on such a Herculean task, but soon it got annoying. Every time we met, she would ramble on about her regimen. Long runs, recovery runs, track workouts, ice baths, GU gels, IT band issues, carb loading – you name it, and she described it all down to the last painful detail. It was a relief when she completed the damn race — in an impressive three hours, no less — something she bragged about for weeks. What I would give to have her back here in our living room telling us about it all over again, as long as she keeps her mouth shut about the Patrick tragedy, of course. While she may have said some terrible things about me towards the end, for the most part she was a good neighbor and a decent person who is missed.

But I doubt she's ever coming back. They found her car parked on a side street across from Hellyer Park. One of the residents on that block reported the abandoned vehicle, stating that it hadn't moved in days. It's officially a missing woman case. The working theory is that Rhonda went there for a run and never returned. The cops and some volunteers are scouring the park and its surroundings for any sign of her.

Based on this development, I'm confident whatever happened to her isn't my fault. It's a relief that I don't have blood on my hands, but I also hate the uncertainty of not knowing her fate and whether she might reappear some day to rat Heather and me out to the cops. Some closure would be comforting.

If Rhonda had been poisoned the way I intended, they would have found her body at home. Even if it took its time to work through her system, they should still have located her by now — either in her car, or on the trail. If she's missing, it means there's been foul play by person or persons unknown. And other than me, who else wanted her to disappear? Only one suspect, and I'm unable to get anything out of her. Heather still refuses to discuss it. In my mind, there are two main possibilities for her silence. Either she's still stuck on my plan B proposal and thinks I'm responsible for Rhonda's disappearance, or she executed plan B herself and is plagued with guilt. I can't decide which is worse.

There's a distance between us now. It hurts. It keeps me up at night. Even Heather's affair and Patrick's tragic end didn't destroy us the way Rhonda is driving a wedge between us. I don't know what to do, but I better figure something out before it's too late.

37

DANIEL

It's still early when there's a knock on the door. My body tingles with dread, like it has been doing every time someone unexpected shows up since Rhonda's disappearance. It's only a matter of time before the cops wise up and come for me. Or Heather.

I take a deep breath and saunter to the door. Five breaths later, I open it. A stern-looking man stands there, and I'd bet a thousand bucks he's a detective. My knees wobble, but I steady myself. *This is it*, I say to myself. *This is the end.*

"Daniel Geraldi?" Bummer. He knows my name, so he's at the right house. The tiny optimist in me had hoped he was at the wrong address and would slink away without causing any trouble. Deep down I'm still crossing my fingers he's not a detective, just an obsessed fan who magically showed up at my door for an autograph or a selfie.

"Yes, that's me."

"Detective O'Brien with SJPD." He extends his hand. I press mine into his firm handshake. "I'd like to ask you some questions, if you don't mind."

A bead of sweat speeds down my back. "What about?"

"I believe you're aware that your neighbor next door, Rhonda Baker's gone missing. We're talking to everyone on the street in case they have anything that can help our investigation."

I'm so nervous, I almost break into a tirade about case priorities like I did with Sanchez. Anything to avoid what's coming next. But that will only buy me so much time. It's better I focus my energies on tackling the situation deftly.

"Step right in." I move aside to make way for him.

He hauls his bulky frame inside. Quite a contrast from wiry Sanchez. I picture them standing together, spitting images of Stan Laurel and Oliver Hardy, and I wonder whether they've ever met, whether they exchange banter like the comedy duo. This stream of thought sparks an idea — I could write a series with a crime-solving pair in the vein of Laurel and Hardy. They'd be bickering and wisecracking their way through murder investigations.

Unbelievable. My life's on fire but my hyperactive author brain refuses to shut off.

We enter the living room. Heather's already waiting, eager to learn if we're in trouble for good this time. O'Brien introduces himself to her and settles onto the couch. The cushions groan in agony. We huddle on the loveseat opposite.

He places his hands on his thighs and lets out a huff. "So, Rhonda was last seen Monday morning getting into her car and driving off in her workout clothes. We reckon she was headed to Hellyer Park for a run as she often did. She never came back. We found her car near the park, but she's still missing."

"Who saw her getting into the car?" I can't resist the question. *Laurie again?*

"Oh, one of the neighbors." He pauses, his eyes locked on mine. *Is he being intentionally vague? Does he think I have something to do with it?* A second bead of sweat races down my back. The way things are going, there'll be a torrent soon. "How was your relationship with Rhonda?"

I was hoping he wouldn't go there. "Cordial enough. She had been reading my books recently. Turned into quite a fan."

"Ah, your books. I've read a couple myself. Entertaining stuff." A smile breaks the surface of his lips. "You gotta brush up on your police procedure, though." He wags a finger at me. The comment stings. I do comprehensive research and try to be authentic, but it's fiction, and I exercise creative license where necessary. Some readers can't handle that.

"I'll keep that in mind. Perhaps you can help me with my next one," I reply, trying to maintain the light mood introduced by this segue into my writing.

O'Brien sits up straighter. "I would love to. Always like to help."

"Thank you."

"Now, about your books. You said she liked them. She didn't make any negative comments? Didn't say she hated your work?"

I furrow my brows, not liking where this man is going. "No. I mean, she wasn't happy about the ending of one of the novels, but she still enjoyed it. Enjoyed it enough to read a second one."

"You sure about that?"

"Yes."

"Because she left a three-star review for ... *Husbands in Peril*, I think it was. Just two days before she disappeared."

Huh. That's news to me. "She did? She didn't tell me about that when we last spoke."

"And when was this?"

"The day before she disappeared."

"And where was this?"

"In her home."

O'Brien glances at Heather, then turns back to me. "You were both there, I assume?"

"No. Only me."

His eyebrows jump up, and he steals another glance at her. "Was this quite common, you visiting Rhonda alone?"

The nerve of this guy!

"Just what are you insinuating, Detective?"

"Nothing. Nothing at all. Now, if you'll answer my question."

"It was the first time. Usually Heather and I go together."

"So why the solo visit? Coincidentally, a day before she disappeared. A day after she left you a three-star review."

"Are you implying I had something to do with her disappearance?" Heather places her hand on mine, silently urging me to calm down. O'Brien notices the gesture and maintains an impassive demeanor. "I get a lot of average and bad reviews. You think I go after all those readers?"

"Ah, but you don't know these other readers personally."

"As I told you earlier, I didn't know she had posted that review. Besides, three stars is not bad at all. It's the ones and twos that are depressing." I pause to catch my breath. "And what exactly do you think I did while I was there? You said yourself she was alive and well when she left the next morning. Clearly, I didn't cause her any harm."

"You have a point." O'Brien clasps his hands together and studies them before raising his gaze. "Now, I also heard things weren't rosy between you two, even long before this review. Something about her dog?"

Damn Bruno! I guess I should come clean.

"It's ... it's just that he licked my hand, and I lost my cool. She wasn't happy about it."

"You bet." I hate the way he's looking at me. Like he's judging me for not going gaga over pets. "So you didn't like her all that much?"

"No! Nothing of the sort. She was a good neighbor. It was just that one incident — which I'm not proud of, by the way. After that she kept Bruno at a distance, but we still talked every now and then. Like I mentioned, she'd started reading my books. I liked her as a person."

O'Brien raises his hands in defeat. "All right, all right. I hear you." Then he turns to Heather. "And you, Mrs. Geraldi. How was your relationship with Rhonda?"

"Friendly. We were almost like sisters. And I adored Bruno."

Love that sisterly touch, Heather. Real smooth.

"I see. Anything either of you could add to help my investigation? Anyone she was on bad terms with? Had she told you she was worried about something?"

Heather and I exchange glances before turning back to O'Brien. No point telling him about that night when Rhonda spied on us. Or the fact that she saw us disposing of a body. "No, nothing of the sort. She seemed happy and breezing through life as usual."

He stands up with an effort. The cushions sigh in relief. "Okay, then. I won't take any more of your time. You have been most helpful." He reaches into his pocket and fishes out a business card. "Here's my card. Do call if you remember anything."

"Sure," we reply in unison, eager to drive him out of the house.

Heather closes the door after he exits and turns, resting her back on the door. "Now that was uncomfortable."

"Tell me about it."

She walks over and wraps her arms around me, kissing me on the lips. It takes me by surprise, but I'm delighted to kiss her back. It's a relief to have things back to normal between us, though I'm not sure what caused this change of heart. Perhaps she realized I couldn't have harmed Rhonda, because I was at home when she disappeared. But a part of me still suspects Heather had something to do with Rhonda's disappearance. This could be a ploy to push that out of my mind. The same way she indulged me while seeing Patrick behind my back. This conflict in my head is driving me crazy. *Do I even know this woman anymore?*

"Eww!" Joyce's voice pulls me out of my thoughts.

"Eww, indeed." Jonas is right behind her. He sounds flat, especially compared to Joyce. His tone reminds me I still haven't had the talk with him.

Before I can ponder over that, Heather whispers in my ear, "Wanna get away?"

"Yes," I whisper back, unable to resist her charms.

She grabs my hand and leads me upstairs. I eagerly follow.

38

ANONYMOUS

I'm a sad, miserable woman. But I wasn't always like this. I had a fantastic childhood, full of love and joy and carefree delights. And ice cream. Lots of ice cream. My teenage years flew by quickly. Adulthood treated me well until Mom and Dad died, dealing me a huge setback, but I survived that, because I'd been blessed with two loving siblings who were always by my side. I adored them both. They gave me the strength to carry on. Until tragedy struck. In the blink of an eye, I lost them too, leaving me grieving, hurting, and asking the question — does the pain ever go away?

Annie was the first to go. My darling little sister. The infant I cradled in my arms the day she was born. She was so tiny, so fragile, that I swore to always protect her. I assisted my mother in feeding her, changing her. As the years went by, I helped Annie walk, taught her how to ride a bicycle, to swim. I guided her with her homework. I was always there for her, as an older sister should be, until I wasn't.

The problems started in her teens. She suffered from bouts of depression, which got worse after our parents passed. I did everything I could to keep things under control, and for a while it seemed like she was stable. Until that fateful day. I shouldn't have let my guard down. I should have been there to protect her, but I failed miserably. Her body in that bathtub — it's an image that will haunt me until the day I die. That afternoon my worst fears were realized as I held her in my arms for the last time. No longer tiny, but still fragile in a way, she still evoked intense emotions inside me like that first time I laid eyes on her.

It was suicide, they concluded. She was troubled, yes, but never once did I imagine she would do something like that. In shock for days, I wondered where I'd gone wrong and what I could have done to prevent this tragedy. *Why would Annie do that?* I asked myself over and over.

And then I found the answer.

There was a book, *Shattered Lives*, sitting right next to the pizza box I'd seen when I'd entered the apartment. I'd never heard of the author, though I was aware of Annie's penchant for thrillers. Curious, I picked it up and flipped through it. She had dog-eared two pages — one of her habits that always annoyed me. All those arguments we had over the years about caring for books, and how she never used the cool bookmarks I bought her. I held the book tight as the tears flowed, wishing I could nag her about it one more time.

I wiped my tears and scanned those pages. There was a high-lighted passage about a girl named Gloria who ends her life by overdosing on fentanyl. The entire process was described in excru-ciating detail, as if it was a handbook for anyone looking for a way out. It couldn't be a coincidence. My innocent little Annie had read it, and it spoke to her, influenced her. She marked the page, and when the time came, she followed through and was lost to me forever. All at the tender age of nineteen.

It was obvious that the author, Daniel Geraldi, was responsible for peddling such nonsense and corrupting impressionable minds like Annie's. There were another eight books by him on her bookshelf. I blamed him for her death and vowed to make him pay. My resolve only grew stronger when I read his other books in an attempt to understand what it was that captivated Annie so.

The depravity! Cheating spouses, people being murdered, and other disgusting and unimaginable things. The man was ruining lives. Now it was not just about Annie anymore — it was about all the families he was destroying with the trash he was churning out. Something had to be done.

My first instinct was to find him and kill him. An eye for an eye, as they say. But that's easier said than done. I realized quite early that I wasn't ready for something like that. Besides, it would be too quick, too light a penalty for his crimes. I would destroy him first, make him suffer and experience the pain that I and, quite likely, others were enduring because of him. Death by a thousand cuts. Besides, a mission like this would keep me busy and help me cope with losing Annie. Perhaps it would prevent me from taking the easy way out like she did.

I used my bereavement leave to spend some time in San Jose, following Daniel and learning more about him. On the surface he seemed like a devoted husband and father, but he was weak enough to leer at women when he thought no one was looking. That sparked the idea of how to reel him in. The book signing presented the perfect opportunity to get the ball rolling. Sylvia Delgado took a break, and Penelope Hayek was born.

I knew I had him the moment he laid eyes on me. Flirting with him was repulsive, but I convinced myself it was okay as long as I didn't have to meet him again. Except for the first picture I sent him, all the others were images I found online. That wasn't my body. The Internet can be a wonderful place sometimes.

Now that I reflect on it, I feel silly about the package. Back then, I saw it as a declaration of war — a sort of warning to Daniel that would inject terror into his life and have him watching his back. The red paint would remind him that he had blood on his hands. Perhaps the package did achieve those goals, but it seems like a meaningless prank now. Quite juvenile, actually. Just goes to show the mushy state of mind I was in back then.

Daniel scared the daylights out of me when he showed up in Sacramento. For an instant I thought I was done for, but I was able to recover my wits and make a dash for it before he got too close. I'm so grateful for friends like Isaac, who watched over me once I told him I was in danger from a lunatic. He sure taught Daniel a lesson by throwing him in jail for a night. Which reminds me, I owe Isaac a nice dinner — maybe more, if things head that way? I blush, surprising myself with this detour in my thoughts. *When was the last time I indulged my romantic side?* All in the past, before Annie died. Maybe I'll be able to heal and get back in the saddle once this is all behind me. Maybe I'll find a new reason to live.

While I was on my revenge spree, I was still grieving and trying to process Annie's death. And then I lost Patrick. My little brother Patrick. I loved him dearly, though he could be a jerk at times. Like when Annie passed. He wasn't as moved as I was by losing his little sister. *Are all men this cold?* I wondered. No, I don't think so — Dad wasn't like that. Patrick was a lovely soul, but he was selfish. He claimed he saw it coming. That he wasn't shocked, because Annie was bound to take her own life someday given her mental state. I don't believe that.

Though I didn't kill Patrick, I am responsible for his demise. If I hadn't recruited him for my mission, he might still be alive today. He didn't want anything to do with my plan, but I convinced him eventually. He moved from Chicago to San Jose for my sake. I would work on destroying Daniel. Patrick would destroy Heather, and by effect, Daniel. She had nothing to do with Annie's death, but she was an enabler by supporting whatever her husband was doing. Besides, learning that Heather had cheated on him would devastate Daniel. Alas, Patrick didn't stick to the plan. He fell in love with the woman. *Why are men so fickle?*

That night at Rancho — I'd intended it to be my first real attack on Daniel, but Heather beat me to it. It was such a rush when she whacked him with the shovel, though I wish she'd finished the job. But I know it couldn't have been easy for her, even in that adrenaline-fueled state.

For a while I thought she was on my side and I should spare her, but the more I zoomed in on her life, the more I concluded she didn't deserve my sympathy, especially after she dumped Patrick and broke his heart. Used him and threw him away like a tissue full of snot. He came to me, sniveling, that night. I reined in the *I told you so* perched on the tip of my tongue, raring to go. But I did remind him not to do anything stupid. Of course, he went ahead and did what he wanted anyway. The things that he did in the aftermath — I had no idea he had planned all that, but it was good stuff, and watching the Geraldis suffer was like a soothing balm.

Until I lost Patrick forever.

I'm convinced Heather had something to do with his death. Daniel, too. The incompetent cops didn't help me, but now it's time for the Geraldis to pay for their sins. Enough of slow torture. I'm ready. Their time has come, and I'm outside their house to ensure they won't hurt anyone again.

But I'm met with an unexpected scene. I watch from the safety of my car as Daniel loads a couple of bags in his Porsche. Heather joins him soon after. Looks like they're leaving for a trip. Bummer. I'd intended to break in and slaughter them both. They wave in the direction of their home. Jonas and Joyce stand by the front door, waving back.

I'm tempted to make a move — force Daniel to experience the agony of losing loved ones, to regret not being there to protect them when they needed him the most. Let him live the rest of his life in misery, shouldering this burden, aching every waking second.

Pulling a baseball cap low over my head, I exit my car as soon as the Geraldis enter theirs and the children return inside the house.

Daniel and Heather are locked in a kiss in the front seat, which allows me to sneak into their backyard through the side entrance. As I'd hoped, the back door is unlocked. I've barely opened it and stepped inside when I freeze. Jonas is staring at me from a few feet away. He's intimidating, with his piercing eyes, his height and muscular build. This was rash. I should have waited until the children disappeared upstairs before entering. It's not like I'm in a hurry. Well, too late.

Before Jonas has a chance to move, I raise my gun and point it at his face. He surprises me by remaining calm. Not a flicker of emotion. If I were in his position, I would have been freaking out. Can I really do this? Can I take an innocent life? I don't have to wait long for the answer, because he steps forward and I squeeze the trigger in response, blowing his head off. At the sight of the blood and gore, my lunch warns me it's planning a trip back up my throat. I distract myself with pleasant thoughts. Like how will Daniel react when he sees my handiwork? Will he weep as he crumples to the ground in anguish? Will he ever find the strength to pick himself up?

Joyce appears out of nowhere and rushes towards Jonas, wailing her heart out. A twinge of regret hits me, because I've caused her immense distress for no fault of her own. But she won't have to suffer for long. I lost two dear ones, and the Geraldis must sacrifice two of their own in return.

Emboldened by my success with Jonas, I return the gun to my pocket and stride up to her. She glares at me with brimming eyes laced with fear. I wrap my hands around her neck and squeeze with all my might. She doesn't resist, as I knew she wouldn't. The shock of losing her brother is overwhelming, and by the time she gathers her wits it will be too late.

The roaring Porsche engine brings me back to my senses. My hands are trembling on the wheel of my car, my body cold and sweaty. Relief floods my being as I watch Jonas and Joyce return inside their home. I didn't do it. I didn't do it. Of course, I didn't. I could never stoop that low. But Daniel and Heather — they do deserve to die. So I start my car and follow them as they ease out of their driveway and speed off.

39

DANIEL

Heather looks radiant today. Happy. Content. As beautiful as the first time I saw her. We're headed to our cabin in Tahoe for a weekend getaway. It's a chance for us to rekindle the flame and rebuild our relationship. No more lies. No more cheating. Complete trust and honesty. And sex. Lots of it. I'm looking forward to it, and so is she.

A little birdie told me that the Patrick investigation has hit a dead end, and Rhonda's disappearance is being linked to Forest Grump. Which means we're in the clear on both fronts. No one can touch us. Even Pen has vanished, finally leaving us in peace. With all this in mind, I suggested we escape, just like we used to when we didn't have a care in the world.

Nothing is perfect, though. I've just loaded the bags in the car when I realize there's one piece of unfinished business. I haven't had the chat with Jonas. It will have to wait until we return.

We speed off in my Boxster, chattering along the way, with long stretches where the only sound is the hum of the engine. The comfortable silence between two souls who have known each other forever. The four-hour drive passes like a breeze, and soon we're at our destination, carrying our bags inside. The sun has ebbed and darkness is taking root. There's a slight chill in the air. I can't wait to settle in front of the fireplace with Heather, wine glass in hand. Kissing, undressing, making love. Slow and sensual at first. Rough and passionate later. I'm grinning as I lock the car and enter the cabin, closing the door behind me.

Heather's in the kitchen opening the bottle of wine. She flashes me a smile as she pours it into the glasses. I amble over and take her in my arms, placing my lips on hers. We might just skip the drinking and move straight to the main course.

Later, once we've satisfied our urges, we're lying on the couch, Heather with her head resting on top of me. She's in a candid mood, sharing her deepest thoughts and desires, the way she did when our relationship was blossoming. I learn that she wants to start running, go to the gym, whip herself back in shape. She promises me she'll only jog around the neighborhood — not on any trails — at least not until Forest Grump is nabbed. She plans on returning to work in real estate again. I'm excited for her — that she's finding a new purpose in life. She has done an amazing job raising the kids. She has made sacrifices. Now it's time for her to live her life. And I'm happy for myself. For us. Hopefully, this is us getting our lives back on track for good.

40

DANIEL

I awake with a start. It's still dark, and confusion reigns for a bit until I realize that I'm at our cabin in Tahoe and not back home. In the sliver of moonlight streaming in through the window I see Heather lying next to me, peaceful. Her bare skin sticks to mine, providing me with comforting warmth. I replay the evening in my head, and my lips part in contentment. Hands down, the best sex of my life. To think that even after all these years and everything we've been through, we still got it.

With those happy thoughts occupying my mind, I close my eyes, only to open them again because I've remembered why I woke up. It wasn't a nightmare this time. There was a noise outside. It's easy to have forgotten, considering how quiet it is now, but I'm sure I heard something. It could be my imagination, or something benign like sounds of the forest, but my guard is up after all the crazy incidents we've experienced in the last few weeks. I would be remiss to ignore it.

I slip out of bed, pulling on my shorts and t-shirt, reminding myself to breathe, and tiptoe out of the room, wishing I had a weapon of some kind to protect myself in case we have an intruder. If I was back home I'd have picked up my baseball bat, but it's slim pickings here. It's dark in the living room, but even with the limited visibility I detect movement. My heart is pounding as my hand searches the wall until I find the switch and turn on the light. A figure stands by the door. The face is familiar, and it sends a surge of terror through me.

"Pen. What are you doing here?"

This is not the beaming, adoring fan I remember from the book signing. Not the flirtatious woman I exchanged emails with. Not even the panicked woman I spotted in Sacramento. She looks cold, emotionless. This is the face of someone who would send a package that explodes and spurts red. The face of someone who would have me rot in jail for no damn reason. *What trouble is she going to cause this time?*

"Not Pen. Sylvia. Sylvia Delgado," she replies with a twisted smile.

Delgado. That name again. And then it dawns on me. "You're ..."

"Patrick's sister."

Her response chills me. My head is swimming. This is a lot worse than I thought. Everything we've been through in the past few weeks, it was all a coordinated attack. Pen and Patrick harassing us until he bit the dust. But why?

"I'm ... I'm sorry for your loss."

"Are you, Daniel? Are you really?" She takes a step towards me, her hatred for me evident in her tone and on her face.

"Yes. I am."

"Why did you kill him, if you really care?"

Oh no. She knows. She knows!

"I didn't kill him. I didn't have anything to do with his death." It's the truth. I hope she sees it that way.

"Perhaps you didn't. But you did haul his body out of your house."

My knees are buckling. It's an effort to stay steady.

"What ... what are you talking about?"

"You know exactly what I'm talking about. Your neighbor saw you and your slutty wife carry Patrick's body out and drive off in his car."

It's like my head will explode any moment. How is this possible? Which neighbor? Did Maisie say something? Or was it Rhonda? But if it was Rhonda, she would have told Sylvia about what happened inside our home as well. And how come Sanchez never found out?

"What neighbor? The cops already interviewed everyone. No one saw anything."

"Well, they did a sloppy job. I, on the other hand, was thorough. This was my brother, after all. One of your neighbors did see you that night. It's just that she didn't realize what she was seeing at the time. By the time that detective went around canvassing, she had flown away on vacation."

She. She said she. Again, Rhonda and Maisie come to mind, but I'm sure neither of them went on vacation recently. Then who is this mysterious neighbor?

"Look, I don't know what she saw, but I assure you, I didn't kill Patrick."

Pen takes another step towards me.

"Your wife then. It must have been her. Why else would you dump the body? First she seduced my brother and got him to a point where he wasn't thinking straight, and when she was done with him, she killed him."

"No. No, Pen. You've got it all wrong. I'm telling you, we had nothing to do with his death." Keep repeating the lie, and eventually everyone will believe it. That's my strategy here. It worked with Sanchez, and I'm hoping it will work with Pen. I'm desperate to keep her at bay, and this is the best I've got to convince her of our innocence.

"So let's assume you didn't cause Patrick any harm. What about Annie?"

"Annie?"

"Yes. Annie."

How does she know about Annie? And then it strikes me — Delgado. I've been so stupid. An imbecile. This explains why Pen looked familiar the first time we met. On closer inspection, I see shades of Annie. It's spooky, like I'm seeing a ghost. If Pen knows what I did to Annie, I'm a dead man.

"I ..."

"How can you write that drivel? Do you even consider what effect your words can have on vulnerable minds?"

"I ... I don't understand."

"Don't act all innocent, Daniel. You know what I'm talking about. You didn't even bother replying to my email. So eager and excited when I was flirting with you, but you clammed up when I raised the important question. Typical shitty male. A lot worse, actually."

She's referring to her email about suicide, of course. I was too chicken to respond, and now it's coming back to haunt me, but I still don't understand how it ties in with Annie.

"My little sister committed suicide after reading *Shattered Lives*. She did it the same way you described it. You're responsible for her death, Daniel. And you're going to pay the price."

The fog of confusion in my head grows for a bit before realization dawns. She doesn't know. All this hatred, all this rage, because she thinks my book led Annie to take her own life. The irony of the situation doesn't escape me. I don't even dare imagine what Pen would do if she discovered the truth.

"I'm sorry." That's all I can muster.

"Sorry is not enough."

"What do you want, then?"

"Your life. And your wife's life. I wanted to torture you. Make you and your family suffer the way Annie suffered. The way Patrick suffered. The way I've hurt this past year. But I'm exhausted, Daniel. I can't do this anymore. This ends tonight."

Panic rises inside me. She's here to kill us. My heart sinks as I think about the kids. After she's done with us, will she slaughter them too? Even if they live, how will they cope once they lose their parents? I can't let this happen. I just can't.

For a moment Pen looked tired. Vulnerable. That was my opportunity to do something, but the time to act has passed, because now she looks as determined as she was before. Nevertheless, I advance towards her, but she's too quick for me. She pulls something out of her jacket.

A gun.

Pointed right at me.

I'm not sure if it's an empty threat — whether the gun is loaded, or how good a shot she is. But her odds are favorable at this distance. I can't take any chances.

"Please … please don't shoot."

"I won't, if you do as I say."

She keeps her weapon aimed at me as her other hand reaches inside her jacket. A pair of handcuffs emerges. She tosses them at me.

"Slip one hand into the cuff."

I do as directed.

"Now take the other one and snap it around the refrigerator handle." She nods in the direction of the kitchen.

"Why …"

"Just do as I say. I can't have you running around while I go say hello to your wife."

"Please … please don't harm her." I'm so nervous that I'm soaked in sweat.

"She's going to pay for what she did to Patrick."

"I'm telling you, she … she didn't kill him. It was an accident." If I can just get through to this woman …

"She's still responsible and deserves what's coming to her."

"Please ..."

"Shut up, Daniel! Such a sissy. Just. Do. As. I. Say."

I shiver as I step towards the fridge, trying not to throw up. This can't be how our lives end.

"What about my kids?"

"Not going to touch them."

That's a relief. But the thought does nothing to cheer me up.

"Now move!"

As I advance towards the fridge, I scan the kitchen, trying to determine whether I'll have any weapons within reach once I'm cuffed. I dare not make any moves while Pen has the gun pointed at me, but I must be prepared to attack any chance I get, which means I must get my hands on something.

It's disappointing. Opening the fridge door might extend my range, but only by so much. The knife rack will still be too far away. Same with the fork drawer. I might be able to get my hands on a pan or two. Then I remember the unfinished bottle of Chardonnay from earlier in the evening that we put in the fridge. I'd be thrilled to smash it on Pen's head. But the cuff's on my right wrist. I wonder how much damage I can inflict with my left hand.

I snap the cuff once I reach the fridge. Pen follows, eager to inspect my work — close enough to confirm that I'm secure, but far enough away that I can't attack her. My heart is thudding. I feel so helpless. Like all those times I stood by as my father attacked Mom.

Satisfied, Pen lowers her weapon and turns towards the bedroom. She is halfway to it when there's movement and Heather crashes into her. She loses her balance and they go tumbling to the other side of the living room. Something clatters — probably the gun slipping out of Pen's hand. The kitchen half-wall blocks my view, but I can hear the struggle. Muffled grunts. The occasional thud. The suspense is killing me. I root for my beloved, praying fervently that she comes out on top.

A scream. It sounds like Heather, and my heart plummets.

"Heather. Heather? You okay?" My voice quivers.

No response. Some more scuffling. Then a primal scream — long and painful. Silence again. I'm desperate to know what happened, but the words don't come out. It's curtains for me if Pen survives this. A part of me is already mourning Heather and skimming through memories of Joyce and Jonas, because I may never see them again.

It's another minute before a figure emerges above the kitchen half-wall. I can't tell who it is because my vision is blurry. I blink a couple of times and release the tears clouding my eyes. A joyous sight. Heather's standing there, bloody and exhausted, but looking alive and well. In her hand she holds a knife.

"The bitch had a knife. She got me with it."

I flinch, not accustomed to hearing such language from Heather. But it's the least of my concerns right now. She's alive, and that's what really matters.

"You alright?" I ask.

"I'll live."

"Is she ..."

"Dead? Yep."

I let out a sigh of relief. We're safe. This nightmare is over. While I wait for my beautiful — and fierce — wife to come over and free me, I realize this is awesome material for my next novel. The first draft is already taking shape in my head, and I'm eager to spit it out once I'm home.

But the excitement fades as I reflect on what happened. Pen was trying to avenge Annie's death. Annie. That innocent, lovely girl who wowed me the first time I laid eyes on her. The beauty who smelled of strawberries and the joys of youth. The way she gazed at me with adoring eyes. The passionate night we spent together. How I was racked with guilt the next morning when I realized I'd failed Heather again. Annie's crestfallen face when I declared it was over between us. How I panicked weeks later when she revealed she was pregnant.

That day when I went to her apartment, still in shock, it's vivid in my mind. She didn't resent me for how I'd treated her. Instead, she was delighted to have me back, relieved to learn that I wanted the baby as much as she did, and that she wouldn't have to abort as I had initially suggested.

The lies came so easily to me. I remember the trusting look on her face as she took a swig of Diet Coke to wash down the pills I gave her, pills I told her were prenatal vitamins, but were in fact laced with fentanyl. She had asked me if they came in gummies, and whether I could get those the next time.

I can still taste the soda on her lips as we kissed, and I can still smell the lavender bath salts as I drew her a bath. I see her stepping in, radiant and glowing, and I see her as she departs this world and slips underwater. I can still feel myself throwing up. I remember the moments after — me cleaning up after myself, ensuring I left no trace behind. And what I did next, what seemed like a stroke of genius back then, but something that backfired disastrously — I took her copy of *Shattered Lives* and highlighted the suicide scene, leaving it on the kitchen counter for someone to find. It was meant to bolster the suicide theory, but it ended up bringing Pen straight to my doorstep.

While I've been haunted since by what I did, the true horror of the heinous crime I committed only sinks in now. All my life I've convinced myself that I'm a good man — flawed, sure, but a good egg, as they say. I've made mistakes, done things I shouldn't have, but I'm a decent human. Now I realize I've been wrong. I'm faced with the stark reality that I'm a terrible, terrible person. A monster. Rotten to the core. I destroyed that innocent girl, shattered her family — and have probably decimated mine too. All because I'm a selfish, self-centered man who must always have it his way. Rhonda was right about that.

What would my father think if he saw me today? He would mock me. I considered myself morally superior to him, but the fact is, I'm a lot worse than him. And Mom — what would she think of me? She would be disappointed and disgusted — ashamed even. My heart sinks at the epiphany, and I'm unable to meet Heather's eyes as she approaches with the gift of freedom.

41

Heather

They say the first one is the hardest. It's not easy to kill a human, but it was for me. At least, the kill was smooth, though the aftermath was difficult to deal with. The image of Patrick lying on the smashed coffee table, bruised and shaken, but very much alive, is still clear in my mind.

I hadn't meant to hurt him. While a part of me hated his guts for the harassment and all the distress he caused me and my family, I still held a soft spot for him in a corner of my heart, an appreciation for the tender moments he granted me when I needed them the most. His actions were simply an immature reaction driven by the passion he held for me, something I tried not to hold against him. But our affair was long dead, so I pushed him away as he tried to kiss me. He stumbled, tripping over the edge of the rug and crashing onto the table. For a moment I froze, not knowing what to do — I was just relieved to get him off me.

The next instant I'd grabbed a shard of glass and sliced his throat. It wasn't until the blood was everywhere and he had breathed his last that I recognized what I'd done, what a crime impetuous

Heather had committed. I curled up on the couch, overcome by shock.

Before long, reality set in — I had to protect myself, and that meant I could not report this incident to the police. I would have to clean up the mess before the children got home. Which meant I needed help. The only ally I had was Daniel, so I called him. *Will I ever be able to unburden myself and confide in him, share what really happened that day?*

It's hard to believe that within the span of a few weeks I've killed two people. I think I'm dealing with this one a lot better. Perhaps that's what they mean when they say the first one is the hardest. It's not like I had a choice this time — it was either Sylvia or me.

Sylvia. A sense of sadness engulfs me. I pity her. I empathize with her. She was only trying to exact revenge for the untimely deaths of her siblings. Wouldn't anyone else in her position do the same, given the lack of justice? And now that she's gone, will anyone mourn her? Does she have any family left? I'm sure she has friends who will miss her, but it's not the same.

I'm exhausted — physically, mentally, emotionally, yearning to discard my burdens and escape to a better life, to a time when I was happy, content, and carefree. Memories flit through my mind. Maternal guilt raises its head as I skip past Joyce and Jonas's early years. Not that I wasn't delighted to have them, but back then I was sleep-deprived and drained — hardly a carefree time.

I stop at my wedding night, Daniel's heat melting me as we cuddle after a session of mind-blowing sex, reveling in marital bliss. But that memory won't cut it — it's tainted by what has happened since. I barrel further through the tunnel of time to one night when I'm eight years old. Dad reads me *Goldilocks and the Three Bears*, and then my parents kiss me goodnight as I lay in bed, my teddy bear, Mr. Snuggles, held tight, the stars on the ceiling throwing soft light. I'm smiling as I shut my eyes. My heart's bursting with joy. That's where I want to be.

But I'm still standing here, bloody and aching, with a knife in hand, studying Daniel. He's patiently waiting for me to rescue him, relieved that this ordeal is over. Instead of rushing to him, I stay rooted to my spot. I'm ashamed, questioning why I overlooked this man's flaws all these years. How did I ignore the brutality of this monster? What does it say about me as a person?

The night I followed him to Rancho, I was furious because I'd learned he was flirting with a woman called Pen. When I saw him standing there, scanning the darkness for her, it enraged me further, and I gave in to my baser instincts by whacking him on the head. I instantly regretted it as he collapsed and curled up in agony. In hindsight, I should have crushed the bastard right there.

But I can't change the past, so I suppress the depressing thoughts and crouch to search Sylvia's pockets. Her front pocket produces a key small enough to fit a handcuff. I palm it and stride towards Daniel. It's not been long, but something has changed. He looks broken. Defeated. Earlier, he had the relieved countenance of a man stranded on an island, eagerly awaiting the approaching ship. Now he looks like he'll readily wade into the water and go under.

I kneel next to him, toying with the key. Before I make my next move, I need some answers. In spite of my sorry state, I feel bold enough to confront him.

"You killed her," I say.

Confusion clouds his face. "Killed who?"

"Annie Delgado."

He replies after a flicker of hesitation. "No, I didn't. You heard Pen. Annie committed suicide."

"First, you *fucked* her." I emphasize the word he so despises. He rewards me with a flinch.

"I ... I did. We already talked about this, remember? And again, I'm sorry."

"You're right. We did talk about your affairs, Daniel. But you didn't tell me she got pregnant."

He flinches again. "I ..."

"She got pregnant, and she wanted to keep the baby."

"Yes, she did."

"So you killed her."

The terror in his eyes is unmistakable. "I didn't," he says softly. It's disconcerting, this calm, because I'd expected a more vocal denial.

"Don't lie to me, Daniel. You purchased fentanyl a few days before she died, and you were in her apartment the day she died."

His eyes widen in surprise. I know all this because I was like a bloodhound once I found out he had cheated on me again. Furious with myself for letting his first indiscretion slide, I kept close tabs on him, wondering how many other flings he had had over the years. Daniel didn't know I was aware of the Post-it in his top drawer which listed all his passwords and allowed me to review his emails.

I followed him to Annie's apartment that day. Of course, I didn't see him do anything — he was careful enough to keep the blinds closed — but between his purchasing the fentanyl and visiting her that fateful day, I put two and two together. I was quite sure of what he had done, but I was in denial. My thoughts were like those of a defense attorney — *it's all circumstantial evidence, where's the proof? You can't prove anything beyond a reasonable doubt!* The fact is, acknowledging his crime made me sick. Besides, it would mean losing the cushy life I was leading. It would also wreck our family, and I couldn't let that happen to my children.

I continue when Daniel doesn't respond. "You poisoned her with the fentanyl, and then you staged it to look like she committed suicide."

He has gone pale, like he's going to pass out at any moment. But he still manages some words. Lies, lies, and damned lies — that's all I expect from him at this point, but he surprises me. I guess he realizes the jig is up.

"She would have destroyed me, Heather. She would have destroyed our marriage and everything I hold dear to me. You understand that, don't you? I couldn't let her do that."

Something shatters inside me. His confession makes his crime real. I can no longer deny the truth. The girl was only nineteen. Just four years older than my Joyce. She made a mistake, and it cost her life. She didn't deserve that. No one does. I imagine what would happen if Joyce was in the same situation. We've put in so much effort to inculcate the right values in our children, to teach them life skills so they can make the right decisions. Even with all that, my daughter could still err. She's human after all. Would she deserve to die?

Rage engulfs me — rage and a strong impulse to act out. But I resist, because I still have questions, and this monster holds the answers.

"You killed Rhonda too."

He looks shocked. *Perhaps it's all an act?* I don't know what to believe anymore.

"I didn't." It's a vehement denial. "I mean I thought about it, yes. Even planned it, and I feel awful about that, but she disappeared before I could follow through." He's staring into my eyes, urging me to believe him. "I ... I thought it was you."

Unbelievable! I'm pissed. *How dare he think I could do something like that?* But I realize his suspicion isn't entirely misplaced. I *am* capable of taking a life. Or two. I'm no better than him. Perhaps we're made for each other in that regard.

"It wasn't me," I say, my voice a whisper.

But as I beat myself up, I think about Annie again and the sheer injustice of it all. It's not the same as me killing Sylvia, or even Patrick. That waif of a girl was harmless. I killed in self-defense.

This time I'm unable to hold back, and impetuous Heather takes over. She slashes the knife across Daniel's throat, closing on what she started that night at Rancho. I stare into his eyes as his life ebbs. The betrayal, the pain, it lurks for an instant, but I feel nothing. And just like that, my husband of twenty-one years is gone.

As I sit beside him, letting it all sink in, I'm overwhelmed with questions. Did I do the right thing? How will I break this to the children? Was I too harsh on him? He was a killer, but so am I. What makes me better than him? The difference, I convince myself yet again, is that he killed an innocent girl.

I can assuage my guilty conscience by claiming that I've slayed the monster. He will never be able to hurt another Annie again. But the fact is, I did turn a blind eye to his misdeeds. It's only once I learned that we would be financially secure even with him gone that I gathered the courage to take action. Sure, his significant income sustains us, but we can survive without it, especially once my career picks up again. And it's not like his royalties will dry up instantly. If anything, his sensational death will lead to a spike in sales. Daniel has socked away enough in a 529 plan to cover college tuition for both children. Besides that, we have over a million dollars in savings and investments. The icing on the cake is the two-million-dollar life insurance policy on him that lists me as the primary beneficiary.

I loved him. Passionately. At least, that's what I convinced myself. It's a huge reason I did everything to make the marriage work. But my straying with Patrick — it was a sign that something was wrong with our relationship. As if I needed any signs after Daniel's flings and what he did to Annie. If I'd heeded the red flags, I would have realized much sooner that, deep down, I didn't love Daniel anymore. That he wasn't worthy of my affection. But now that

I've seen the light, I won't miss the philanderer, the cold-blooded killer. The children will, though, and that cuts deep.

I drift back to the present and the delicate situation. This time I don't have Daniel to help me out. I must handle this mess by myself. I replay the story in my mind. Sylvia broke into the cabin and attacked him, killing him in the process. Her motive? *I have no clue, Officer.* Then she came for me, but I managed to kill her. *It was self-defense, Officer.* Simple enough if I play my part right.

I turn to Daniel's lifeless body and stare hard, forcing myself to revisit all the memorable moments we had together, to remind myself of what I've lost. Those early days of our courtship. The night he proposed, eagerly awaiting my response as he knelt before me. Our wedding day. The honeymoon. All our vacations, with both of us at our best, relaxed and stress-free. The tender nights in bed. The passionate encounters. The birth of our children. The joy we shared as they hit each milestone. Countless more vignettes of our life as a couple, some memories I'd even forgotten existed. It works. The dam breaks and I'm bawling. I dial 911, confident that I sound distressed enough.

42

DETECTIVE SANCHEZ

Detective Sanchez is seated on his couch mulling over the day and the past few months in general. It's been a rough time, especially in light of the tragedy in Tahoe. Sylvia Delgado's untimely death has shaken him. Sometimes he feels responsible, because if he had nabbed Patrick's killer, she would not have ventured out for vigilante justice and lost her life. But there are times where he questions whether he could have done anything at all. Perhaps Sylvia was not quite right in the head, and her accusations regarding the Geraldis were unfounded. It could be something that runs in the family. After all, hadn't her sister committed suicide after being depressed for a while? And hadn't her brother's behavior been ... odd?

The Tahoe tragedy is under investigation. Sanchez is not on the case, since it's out of his jurisdiction, but the local authorities have talked to him multiple times after learning about the cases connecting the people involved. They are of the opinion that Sylvia was the perpetrator, and the Geraldis the victims. Quite likely that is the case.

He feels for Heather Geraldi and her family. She lost her husband, and her children, their father. Devastating circumstances. In fact, he was at their home today, not in an official capacity, but to offer his condolences. She was still in mourning. The children weren't doing much better, as far as he could tell. Of course, he couldn't resist probing a bit, trying to uncover the truth — to determine whether she's as innocent as she pretends to be. Heather caught on quick and dodged his queries like a pro. There was that one moment, when she handed him his coffee, her hand grazing his, that glint in her eye — perhaps he had imagined it, but it convinced him she was not a victim, perhaps she wasn't in mourning at all. *Had she made a pass at him?* It would make sense if she wanted to distract him and lure him away from the ugly truth.

He has an urge to dig deeper, to investigate further, but he reminds himself it's not his case. The old Sanchez — the Sanchez before Trish left — would have gone crazy trying to get to the bottom of it. But the new Sanchez — Sanchez 2.0, as he likes to call himself — has pledged that he will not overwork. After all, what did that get him? He's tired of vacillating between his role of dedicated cop, following his duty to protect the people and nab criminals no matter what the personal cost, and his belief that this is just another job, and he's entitled to an appropriate work-life balance, that he deserves to prioritize his mental and physical health — and his relationships. He lost Trish in the process, and he can't — won't — risk losing more.

Besides, he has a date tonight. A real live date. They've exchanged a few messages online, and he has a positive feeling about this woman. He's nervous. He's excited. He wants to make a strong impression. It's the first time since Trish. A quick hot shower to wash off the filth from the Geraldis and the Delgados, and he'll be a new man, ready to meet the woman of his dreams. At least, that's what he hopes.

Epilogue

It's been three months since Daniel's death. The investigation around the circumstances has died down. Heather's version of events has been accepted by the authorities. In the meantime, Rhonda's body has been found. They've nabbed the killer, too. She was his seventh victim. Heather was relieved to learn that Daniel had nothing to do with it, but she grieves for her friend and neighbor in a way she wasn't able to grieve for her husband.

Jonas's heart still aches. He misses his father. His best friend. His hiking buddy. The man who taught him to ride a bike and drive a car. He wishes he could sit with Daniel once again, both of them sipping iced teas, and just talk. Jonas would tell him about Rhonda's killer — that he's an Asian man in his mid-fifties — that Daniel's guess was so far off-base. That the killer randomly abducted the women, keeping them locked up, watching them and talking to them for days before poisoning them and burying them in his backyard. They would speculate about his motives and how he targeted his victims, both of which are still unknown.

Daniel would take a sip of his drink and mock the killer's sloppiness in letting the eighth woman kick him in the groin and escape.

That must have hurt, Jonas would have remarked. They would laugh, and they would move on to other topics.

Some day in the future he would have sat down with his father sipping Macallan rather than iced tea. At least, that's what Daniel had promised him — *as soon as you turn twenty-one*, he had said. Now fate has robbed Jonas of that opportunity, and he stands in the kitchen, burdened with this painful knowledge, firing up the coffee maker.

"You're up early," says Heather as she enters the kitchen.

He turns to face her. "Yeah, I couldn't sleep."

It's just the two of them. Joyce is at a sleepover at her friend's place and will be back later that afternoon. She has taken Bruno with her. The Geraldis adopted him after Rhonda's death was official. Laurie didn't mind at all.

"Are you okay?" Heather asks, concern writ on her face.

"Yes."

"You miss him, don't you?"

Jonas nods.

"Me too."

It's an exchange they've had several times in the past few weeks. He studies her face. After all this time he isn't sure whether it's an act or she really misses her husband. Whether she genuinely did care about Daniel. Jonas turns back to the counter and fills a mug with coffee. He hands it to her.

"Oh, thank you." She sounds surprised, which is not unexpected since he has never made her coffee. She settles into the breakfast nook and takes a sip. "This is good."

"Thanks." He pauses to study her for a few seconds more. "I'll be back."

He sprints up the stairs. He was up late last night, prepping for this important day. Reviewing everything one final time, he confirms that it's all as it should be before heading back downstairs. Heather is still sipping her drink.

"What would you like for breakfast?" he asks.

She's slow to react, but she eventually raises an eyebrow. "To what do I owe this honor? Mother's Day is still far away, and as far as I can remember, it's not my birthday either."

Jonas shrugs. "Just."

"Pancakes would be nice. Banana pancakes. With chocolate chips."

"Banana chocolate chip pancakes coming right up, Señora."

She smiles, a wistful look in her eyes. "You know, this is what your father made for me the first time we ..."

"Mom! Stop!" He senses where this is going and wants to avoid the embarrassment. He has heard this story before.

"Oh, come on, you're an adult now. Humor me a bit. He took me out to dinner. Our third date. We ended up at his place and ... our first time together." Heather pauses, the goofy smile still plastered on her face. "I loved him, you know. I really did."

Jonas detects a pang of guilt coming on, some doubt too, and he tries to ward it off by busying himself. He takes out a mixing bowl and works on the ingredients while a pan heats up on the range. Whole wheat flour and baking powder first, followed by a mashed banana. He cracks an egg and empties it into the bowl. Some milk, and then he mixes, tossing some chocolate chips into the batter. A tear emerges from his eye and flows down his cheek. It's as if Daniel is by his side, guiding him on how to prepare the perfect pancake.

"I was alone in bed when I woke up the next morning. I walked over to the kitchen. It was a little place — a one-bedroom apartment, but he maintained it immaculately. That's one of the things I liked about him." She has a faraway look in her eyes, and her eyelids are heavy now. "Anyway, so he was mixing the batter, just like you are now."

Jonas ignores the comment and continues. He wishes he was doing something noisy, like working with the blender so that he could drown out Heather's voice. Once the batter is ready, he starts cooking the pancakes. His mind wanders through his life so far, through his childhood and all the way down to his first memories. How Heather would smother him with hugs and kisses. The times he was sick and she comforted him. All the delicious meals she served him. She loves him, cares for him. He's sure of that. But what she did to Daniel — it was wrong. Unforgivable.

"They were delicious. The best I'd ever had. I ..."

Jonas doesn't react to the abrupt silence. It's a relief to his ears. He continues cooking, and soon he has a good-sized stack. Dropping a cube of butter on it, he grabs the bottle of maple syrup and smothers the pancakes in gooey sweetness. Then he takes the plate over to join Heather.

Her coffee mug is on the table, empty. She's still on the chair, her head resting on the table next to the mug. He grins from ear to ear as he digs into his breakfast. It's been a rough few weeks.

It's not fair, he thinks, that she survived Sylvia's attack but his innocent father perished. In his mind, she doesn't deserve to live on, considering how she had sinned with Patrick — how she had cheated on his father and started this whole mess.

Jonas was at the motel to pick up a supply of weed from his dealer when he spotted her. Sheer luck. It's quite unfortunate that he learned about his mother's infidelity but is oblivious to his father's frailties. Perhaps things would have ended differently if he had been better informed. He believes he has exacted revenge on Daniel's behalf and has meted out the punishment Heather deserves. As Daniel's biggest fan, he has read every novel published by his hero. He knows how this is done.

For a fleeting moment Jonas worries about Joyce. She'll be devastated. First she lost Patrick. Then her father. Losing her mother so soon after could wipe her out. But he'll take care of her. His little sister. She'll be much better for it in the long run. A characterless mother like Heather is a terrible role model for a teenage girl.

Done with his pancakes, he picks up his plate and heads to the kitchen. He rinses the plate and the pan, placing both in the dishwasher. Then he ambles back to Heather and carries her lifeless form up the stairs. After settling her in her bed, he returns for the mug. He wipes the exterior clean and presses her fingers on it in various spots so that only her fingerprints are on it. He places the mug on top of the sheet of paper that lies on her nightstand. *I can't take it anymore.* That's all it says. A brief suicide note Jonas wrote up in his mother's handwriting. He had planned on a more detailed letter, but in the end he decided the simpler the better. Less room for mistakes on his part.

He checks Heather's pulse. Nothing. She's not breathing either. Pleased with his handiwork, he walks over to his room and crashes into bed. He'll sleep a few hours before "discovering" that his mother is no more. Then he'll call 911, sounding distressed like any boy worried about his mother. The subsequent investigation will go much smoother for him if the authorities learn that he woke up at his usual time, and he wasn't around when she ended things. Joyce will confirm that he indeed sleeps in most mornings. She might express shock that Heather took this step, claiming that her mother was coping fine and was far from depressed, but he'll convince the cops that he has been concerned about Heather for a while now. He'll tell them she was disturbed, that she had been hiding it from Joyce, not wanting to worry her fragile daughter.

It's almost two years since Daniel murdered Annie and staged it to look like suicide. Without knowing it, Jonas has followed in his father's footsteps. As they say, the apple doesn't fall far from the tree. But while Daniel had been unable to sleep for a week afterwards and was haunted by his horrific crime until his last breath, Jonas sleeps content — the deep sleep of one satisfied by a job well done.

THANK YOU!

Dear reader,

Thank you for reading *Shattered Lives*! If you enjoyed this book, please post a review on your favorite platforms. Reviews help more readers find me and my books, so a positive review can be very helpful and is immensely appreciated.

To learn more about me and my work, visit https://www.vineetvermaauthor.com. You can also sign up for my newsletter there to receive the latest updates about my writing, get book recommendations, and follow links to cool book promos. If you prefer social media, you can follow me here:

Facebook: @VineetVermaAuthor

Instagram: @vineetvermaauthor

X: @VineetvAuthor

polished and pristine exterior. From jealous ex-lovers to rival tech giants, Jay has created powerful enemies, all of whom would be happy to see him dead--and all of whom have solid alibis. White and Conley hit dead end after dead end. And when blackmail schemes and copycat murders come into play, finding the killer becomes increasingly more urgent. Can they catch a break, or will a murderer go free in Silicon Valley?

books2read.com/u/3JXAWA

"Devious Minds is a must-read for fans of short fiction looking for stories with dark themes, shocking twists, and insights into the criminal mind."

When you hear the word "criminal", what comes to mind? A cold-blooded killer? A professional burglar? Perhaps someone peddling drugs? People who indulge in illegal activities everyday.

But sometimes it's just regular Joes like you and me. Men and women who do honest work, staying within the limits of the law, until one day they can't take it anymore and they commit a crime. But what is it that makes them crack? Was there something devious always lurking under the surface, waiting to emerge?

Devious Minds is a collection of crime stories, including police procedurals, psychological thrillers, and more that will suck you into a world of mystery and suspense. Fasten your seat belt and enjoy the ride!

https://books2read.com/u/47WjdA

ABOUT THE AUTHOR

Vineet is a tech professional by day and has been a lifelong fan of mysteries, be it in books or on screen. He enjoys writing and creating a world of suspense that leaves his readers guessing until the end. With his debut novel, *Barefoot in the Parking Lot*, and the follow up short story, *The Stick*, he fulfilled his dream of becoming a published author. He lives in San Jose, California with his wife and twin boys and hopes to keep plumbing the depths of his twisted mind to write for years to come.

9 781736 401743